"Oh, my God. [...]
fertility clinic [...]

"What is it?" Dr. R[...]

"The note you found—it's in Sarah's writing. She covered for me when I went on break. It's a change in appointments. Wentworth canceled and Langdon took her place."

"Wentworth? Wasn't she supposed to receive Jared Steele's sperm?"

"Yes. He was here this afternoon." The receptionist picked up a folder marked Wentworth. "Just as I thought. These forms are all signed by *Lisa Langdon.* She and Mr. Steele were talking. I thought they were together...."

"Are you saying Miss Langdon was inseminated with Mr. Steele's sperm?"

The receptionist nodded. "What are we going to do?"

Dr. Rubin sighed. "We wait until Miss Langdon comes in for her follow-up appointment. Once we know the results of conception, then we'll tell them what happened. But I hate to imagine what's going to happen when two strangers find out they both want the same baby...."

Dear Reader,

Summer is a time for backyard barbecues and fun family gatherings. But with all the running around you'll be doing, don't forget to make time for yourself. And there's no better way to escape than with a Special Edition novel. Each month we offer six brand-new romances about people just like you—trying to find the perfect balance between life, career, family, romance....

To start, pick up *Hunter's Woman* by bestselling author Lindsay McKenna. Continuing her riveting MORGAN'S MERCENARIES: THE HUNTERS series, she pairs a strong-willed THAT SPECIAL WOMAN! with the ruggedly handsome soldier who loved her once—and is determined to win her back!

Every woman longs to be noticed for her true beauty—and the heroine of Joan Elliott Pickart's latest book, *The Irresistible Mr. Sinclair,* is no different; this novel features another wonderful hero in the author's exciting cross-line miniseries with Silhouette Desire, THE BACHELOR BET. And for those hankering to return to the beloved Western land that Myrna Temte takes us to in her HEARTS OF WYOMING series, don't miss *The Gal Who Took the West.*

And it's family that brings the next three couples together—a baby on the way in *Penny Parker's Pregnant!* by Stella Bagwell, the next installment in her TWINS ON THE DOORSTEP series that began in Silhouette Romance and will return there in January 2000; adorable twins in Robin Lee Hatcher's *Taking Care of the Twins;* and a millionaire's heir-to-be in talented new author Teresa Carpenter's *The Baby Due Date.*

I hope you enjoy these six emotional must-reads written *by* women like you, *for* women like you!

Sincerely,

Karen Taylor Richman
Senior Editor

Please address questions and book requests to:
Silhouette Reader Service
U.S.: 3010 Walden Ave., P.O. Box 1325, Buffalo, NY 14269
Canadian: P.O. Box 609, Fort Erie, Ont. L2A 5X3

TERESA CARPENTER

THE BABY DUE DATE

Silhouette®

SPECIAL ✦ EDITION®

Published by Silhouette Books

America's Publisher of Contemporary Romance

Thank you to my family, friends and critique partners for
having faith and helping to make this book possible.

Thanks, Mom and Dad, Kathy, Christy, Mike,
Mary and Brandon. I love you all.

To my critique buddies past—Dawn, Jean, Virginia and
Marce—and present—Jill, Jackie, Terry, Sandy, Marilyn and
Diana—for always demanding the best from me.

 SILHOUETTE BOOKS

ISBN 0-373-24260-3

THE BABY DUE DATE

Copyright © 1999 by Teresa Carpenter

Visit us at www.romance.net

Printed in U.S.A.

TERESA CARPENTER

is a fifth-generation Californian who currently lives amid the chaos of her family in San Diego, CA. She loves living in San Diego because she can travel for thirty minutes and be either in the mountains or at the beach. She began her love affair with romances in the seventh grade when she talked her mother into buying her her first category romance; they've been together ever since.

Teresa has worked in the banking/mortgage industry for fifteen years. When not working or writing, she likes to spend time with her nieces and nephew, go to the movies and read.

A member of RWA/San Diego, she has participated on the chapter board in numerous positions, including president, VP Programs, newsletter editor and conference coordinator. She is especially proud of having received the chapter's prestigious Barbara Faith award.

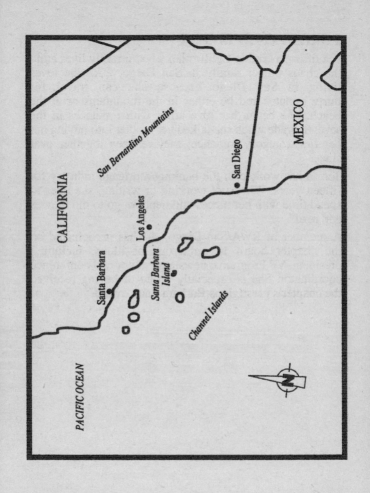

Prologue

Dr. Clarice Rubin stepped up to the reception desk of the San Diego Fertility Clinic and held out a slip of paper to the receptionist. "I found this note with the documents you put on my desk."

"Thank you." The receptionist accepted the note and gave it a casual glance.

Preoccupied with other thoughts, Dr. Rubin started to turn away. She stopped when she saw the other woman's expression become dismayed.

"Oh my God."

"What is it?" Dr. Rubin demanded.

"This is Sarah's writing. She covered for me while I went on break. It's a change in appointment. Wentworth canceled and Langdon took her place. Sarah must have made the arrangements before she went home ill this morning."

"Wentworth? Isn't that the woman who was supposed to receive Jared Steele's specimen?"

"Yes. He was here this afternoon." As she spoke, the receptionist picked up a folder marked Wentworth. "Just as I thought, these forms are all signed by Lisa Langdon. She and Mr. Steele were talking. I thought they were together." Her voice rose in agitation.

"Are you saying Miss Langdon was impregnated with Mr. Steele's sperm?"

The receptionist nodded. "It was a direct transfer."

"Sweet heavens." All the ramifications of the mix-up ran together in Dr. Rubin's mind, not least of which was Jared Steele's reaction when he heard the news.

"What are we going to do?"

"It was an honest mistake." She sighed, knowing that made little difference. "When is Miss Langdon's follow-up appointment?"

The receptionist flipped through some computer pages. "In two weeks, on April 18."

"We wait. For two weeks. Once we know the results of conception, I'll call Jared Steele and explain the situation."

"What about Miss Langdon?"

"I'll have to tell her, too. And the lawyers. What a mess. I must say, I hope this is one time nature favors the odds and the insemination doesn't take the first time. I hate to imagine what's going to happen when two strangers find out they both want the same baby."

Chapter One

"Congratulations, Lisa, you're pregnant." Dr. Rubin's words echoed in Lisa Langdon's mind as she pushed open both doors of the San Diego Fertility Clinic and stepped outside into the bright mid-April sunshine.

She was going to have a baby!

She felt excited and pleased. Pleased? No, that was much too mild for such an on-top-of-the-world feeling. She headed over to her Nissan, opened the car door and slipped into her seat. Elated was a better word, or exhilarated, or even overwhelmed.

Before contacting the clinic, she'd forced herself to consider the consequences of her actions. She couldn't deny the obvious ticktock of her biological clock or the wish to end her loneliness. But beyond those surface desires were deeper needs. She had so much to give a child—intelligence, talent, love.

Lots and lots of love.

Since making her decision, she'd experienced a sense of purpose. She knew she'd make a good mother.

"I'm pregnant." She said the words aloud for the first time, her voice filled with awe. "I'm going to be a mommy."

Taking deep breaths, Lisa forced herself to calm down. She looked to where her hands instinctively cradled her lower abdomen, the resting place of her child. Again, the wonder of her condition flooded through her. She had to consciously relax the protective hold before she could insert her key and put the car in gear.

As she pulled out of the parking lot, she reflected on a saying her mother used to quote, "Each day is a new beginning." The statement inspired hope and offered promise. She remembered it now as she had so many times in the past. Always before she'd used the saying and the memory of her mother to buoy her spirits. Today was different. She'd done something special in conceiving this child. She'd *created* hope and promise for the future.

Suddenly fear sent an icy shiver down her spine. She rubbed her arms to dispel the chill.

She wouldn't allow Dr. Rubin's other, disturbing news to detract from the specialness of the moment.

Jared Steele was going to be a father.

Stunned, he hung up the phone and leaned back in his huge executive chair in his elegantly appointed office. He'd been prepared for the news from Dr. Rubin, of course. He'd been waiting to hear confirmation of the fact for the past two weeks.

He was going to be a father.

Running a hand through his hair, he realized he wasn't prepared at all. He felt torn. While part of him experienced relief, pleasure, excitement, the other part of him saw the problems ahead. Fear, anger and the anxious sensation of being out of control swamped him.

He pushed away from his chair, seeking action as a cure for his inner turmoil.

"Get me Zack," he demanded of his secretary.

Jared waited, impatiently pacing from his desk to the window and back again.

How had the error happened? He'd planned everything so carefully, down to the last detail. Disappointment twisted in his gut. How could everything have gone so wrong?

"You yelled?" Zack Farrell entered the room after a brief knock.

"Where have you been?" Jared snapped.

"I was down the hall," Zack said, closing the door behind him. "What's the problem?"

"You won't believe what's happened."

"So tell me," Zack commented, sinking into a chair.

Jared waited by the window while his security executive settled into his seat. "Comfortable?" he asked caustically, then cursed himself for taking his bad mood out on his friend.

Zack merely inclined his head. "I've worked for you for seven years. We've been friends for longer than that. When you're in this kind of mood, a man may as well make himself comfortable."

Jared frowned but didn't argue. He knew the truth when he heard it. He knew, too, that Zack would understand when he heard Jared's news. The good and the bad.

"The surrogate agency called this morning. Wentworth skipped. She never made it to the clinic. She lied about keeping the appointment then took the advance money and ran."

"Tough luck. Do you intend to replace her?"

"The problem's not that simple." Jared wished the situation was so easy to resolve. Though he doubted he'd elect to go through the process again. There was no way to explain how the procedure had affected him. And to find out that such a vital part of himself had moved beyond his reach, beyond his control, made him feel helpless and demoralized.

"Dr. Rubin also called. When Wentworth canceled, one of the nurses rescheduled someone else for that time. Then the nurse went home ill. Without telling anyone about the change."

"So you're saying—"

Jared drew in a deep breath, then a grin broke over his face as the excitement rushed back. "I'm going to be a father."

An answering smile lit Zack's dark gaze. He stood and grasped Jared's arm for a hearty shake, his other arm wrapped around Jared's shoulder, and pounded him on the back. "Congratulations, you old stud."

"Thanks." Jared broke the contact then sat on the edge of his desk. "But there's more."

"More?" Zack resumed his seat. "What? Twins?"

Twins? Jared couldn't even comprehend the thought. Right now, he needed to worry about getting one baby back.

"A strange woman is walking around out there with my child inside her!"

That was what tore at Jared. Not that his plans were destroyed or that he'd lost control of the situation. But the thought that a child of his existed. A child who may forever be beyond his reach.

He couldn't tolerate that, not again.

"Settle down, Jared, the chances are—"

"Don't quote me statistics, damn it. I need to know what to do."

Zack looked surprised. "You're asking me?"

"I'm desperate." Jared sighed, combing his fingers through the mahogany strands of his hair.

"Write it off," Zack advised. "Contact the agency and start over from scratch."

"Are you crazy?" Jared glared. "I can't spend the rest of my life knowing I have a child running around somewhere. Could you?"

"No, but we aren't talking about me. To forget the whole thing ever occurred would be the simplest solution."

Jared stepped behind the desk and lowered his length into the oversized executive chair. "When have you ever known me to take the easy way out of anything?"

"There's always a first time."

"Well, this isn't it. I can't believe you're suggesting I ignore my child's existence. It would defeat my every motive for choosing to have a baby."

"I've never been real clear on why you decided to go this route. A man can avoid his mother's matchmaking attempts without resorting to artificial insemination to provide her with grandchildren."

Jared eyed his friend. "You can say that with a straight face after Saturday night?"

A rare grin flashed across Zack's features. "The two ladies involved aren't blaming your mother. They believed the invitations came from you. For future reference, you should tell your mother it's best not to book two women for the same night." A chuckle accompanied the advice.

"Very funny. I don't recall you laughing quite so

loud when Mother recruited you to handle the overflow on Saturday.''

"That's because I didn't like the look in her eye. Too much speculation. What's the deal, Jared? Your mother wouldn't have made a mistake like that a year ago.''

"I know." With Zack, Jared didn't attempt to hide his concern. They'd been friends too long. Zack knew his mother too well. "Maybe now you'll understand my worry. My mother is the consummate hostess. Hell, it's been her profession for the past forty years. For her to make such a mistake—''

Jared shook his head. His mother was a beautiful, vital woman. Always, he'd been proud of her. He'd been saddened over the past year to watch her lose her usual zest. Since his sister, Mary, had moved out, his mother had changed before his eyes. "Dr. Rubin called it the empty nest syndrome.''

"Was this before or after your discussion about modern fertility practices?''

The question reminded Jared of his more immediate problem. He frowned. "I didn't decide to have a baby because of my mother, though I admit I hope she'll benefit as well. The point is, I'll never marry." Not after his disastrous engagement. Not after the betrayal and loss he'd suffered. He'd learned his lesson. "But I don't see why that should prevent me from having a family. I have a lot to offer to a child. This corporation is a hell of an inheritance.''

And he'd hoped the sense of emptiness and guilt would finally be put to rest.

Jared looked his friend straight in the eye, knowing what he would be asking of him. "I need you to do something for me. Find out who the woman is, Zack. I want to know everything about her, name, address, occupation, date of birth, what type of toothpaste she uses. Everything.''

Zack simply stared at Jared with expressionless black eyes.

Jared met him stare for stare. This was too important for him to suffer qualms about bending the law. As an ex-government agent, Zack knew how to find the woman, how to get hold of the information Jared required.

"It's that important to you?" Zack didn't ask the question lightly.

"Yes." Jared resented the situation that demanded he ask this of his friend. It was a sign of his desperation that he did so anyway.

"I'll look into it. Can you give me anything to go on?"

"Not much. I met a woman at the clinic. Slim, about five-five, five-six in heels, blond hair pulled back in one of those complicated braids. Pretty eyes, an unusual color, like antique gold. She was the only other person I saw, so the timing is right.''

"That's a detailed description for a brief encounter. What made you notice her? She sounds too innocent to be your type.''

Jared shrugged. "She talked to me. That's right," he said, remembering the conversation. "I caught her staring at me. She apologized, said she was an artist. Told me she liked my nose.''

"Your nose?"

He sent Zack a quelling glance. "She was the kind of person you remember.''

"Why?" Zack's gaze held intense interest.

"Because she looked you in the eye, and when she smiled, you knew it was for you and not just to meet the occasion.'' Jared searched his mind for further details. ''She said Dr. Rubin had some of her work.''

In a deceptively graceful movement, Zack rose to his feet. ''I've had less to go on. Give me a week.'' He headed for the door.

''Zack?'' Jared waited until Zack turned to face him. ''Thanks.''

''Ashley, oh, Ashley, it's really happening.'' Feeling her throat close around the words, Lisa grasped the phone in both hands and snuggled into the corner of her peach floral couch. She wished with all her heart that Ashley Todd, Lisa's best friend and agent, was in San Diego not New York so they could hug and dance and celebrate.

''I'm so happy for you, little mama. As soon as I get home, we're going out. Have you told them at the gallery yet?''

''No, I want to wait until I'm further along.'' She laughed with sheer joy. ''I have eight and a half months to go. I just want to hug the news to myself for a while, except for my best friend, of course.'' She swallowed hard and pushed away the dark thoughts of another's claim. ''I guess I'm superstitious and don't want to jinx anything.''

''What's wrong, Lisa?'' Concern sounded down the line in Ashley's voice.

''Nothing.'' Lisa let the excitement swell through her and across the line, convincing Ashley, convincing herself. ''Everything is perfect. Or will be when you get home and we can celebrate.''

''It's a date. I'll be back in San Diego in a week. Take care of yourself, and the baby.''

''Believe me, I will, this baby is the most important thing in the world to me.''

Jared stared down at the leather portfolio Zack had given him. Finally. It had taken nearly a week. Six days, every second an eternity. Zack was good, but he hadn't even had a name to start with. Now he did.

With mixed emotions, Jared flipped open the file. Lisa Langdon's face stared back at him. He lifted the picture. If memory served him well, it was an excellent likeness. The photograph showed to advantage the blond wisps of her hair. Gleaming with the brilliance of sunlight, the thick, waist-length strands were secured in a braid. Loose tendrils escaped to frame her face. Her ivory skin glowed with health and vitality. A natural blush colored the high line of her cheekbones.

Zack was right, she wasn't his type at all. He preferred sophisticated beauty to wholesome prettiness.

He flipped through the file and began to read. Now thirty, she'd been orphaned at the age of ten and grown up in foster homes. She currently held the position of bookkeeper at a prestigious gallery, but dedicated all her leisure time to painting.

Her social life particularly interested him. According to Zack's report, her dating habits had changed drastically in the recent past. At first she'd dated sporadically, but over the last year, she'd begun going out frequently, meeting and dating a variety of men. The pattern altered in January with her first visit to the clinic, tapering off completely.

"Facts." Frustrated disgust rang through the word. How was it possible to know so much about a woman, and yet not know anything about her?

He looked again at her picture. Her smile flashed an invitation to share in her genuine enjoyment of life. That genuineness caught a man's attention, tempted him to explore further until he became trapped by the allure of her eyes. Looking into the golden depths,

Jared saw a clear pathway to her soul, which appeared honest and pure, unclouded by secrets or self-doubt.

That kind of openness could lure a man to give of himself, to trust. To protect her at all cost, even against himself.

Of course, he told himself as he rose to pace the room, it was only his imagination or a distortion in the photograph created with clever lighting.

Dr. Rubin had his name, address and phone number; he'd made her promise to give the information to Miss Langdon. But that had been a week ago. He'd been waiting for the phone to ring ever since.

He drew a deep breath then ran a smoothing hand over the dark thickness of his hair, attempting to bring himself under control. She'd need time, he knew that, time to absorb the news. Anybody would.

But she'd had a week, darn it.

"This isn't going to work." Ten minutes later, Jared voiced his aggravation. "I don't know who I think I'm fooling." He stopped pacing long enough to stare out the picture window. "I'm not going to be able to sit here and wait while she casually decides on my future, my child's future. What if she never calls?"

Impatient, he swung back into the room and glared at the silent telephone. "God, I'm talking to myself. What better proof do I need?"

He couldn't wait any longer, not for something this important. He'd never been the type to sit still while important decisions were being made regarding his life. And he couldn't forget the past and what had happened the last time he hadn't had control.

"I won't exert any undue pressure," he promised himself. "I'll just be there to help her go through the facts."

He felt better now that he had a planned course of action. On his way out, he asked his secretary to clear his calendar of all appointments. He would not be back today.

Chapter Two

Lisa's car sighed to a stop in her driveway. She'd just come from an early celebration dinner with Ashley, who'd flown in from New York this afternoon. Lisa was still flying high on excitement and joy and finally being able to share her feelings with someone she cared about. She gathered together her things, including a fluffy white teddy bear Ashley had given her, then headed up the stone walkway.

Lisa smiled, remembering Ashley's enthusiasm. She was almost as thrilled about the baby as Lisa was.

Head bowed, she dug through her purse in search of her house keys, which were playing elusive games. She headed up the walkway toward the porch of her home, an older cottage squeezed between two Mount Helix estates.

"Finally." Lisa's fingers curled around the ragged edge of the keys. Having located them, she raised her attention from her purse and came to a dead stop.

A man stood directly in her path.

"Oh." Surprised, she lost her grip on the keys, and they fell to the ground. Instinctively, she stooped to pick them up.

A pair of shining leather loafers topped by finely creased pin-striped pants came into her line of vision. Her gaze followed the creases up to eye level. He shifted impatiently, widening his stance and sweeping his jacket behind his wrists to shove his hands into the pockets of the slacks he wore. The fabric pulled taut across muscular thighs.

Quickly, Lisa pushed to her feet. She confronted a silk-clad torso, the white shirt emphasizing the expanse of a broad chest. Who? she wondered, noting the boldly chiseled, sensuous mouth, her curiosity growing when she encountered a perfectly proportioned nose.

Then it clicked. The man from the fertility clinic.

"Jared Steele." Recognition made her wary as she met his clear blue gaze.

Abruptly she stepped back, her hands falling to shield her lower abdomen. Why was he here? Stupid question. She should have expected him before now. He was here because of the baby. Her baby.

"Yes," Jared acknowledged. "I've been waiting for your call." He stood still, not advancing, not retreating.

Still, she took a distancing step back. "How did you know where I live? Dr. Rubin assured me she hadn't released that information."

"She didn't." He made a vague, negative gesture.

Lisa flinched. All her senses screamed at her to retreat farther. He'd never known what it cost her to stand her ground.

He frowned. "Look, can we go inside? We need to talk."

She shook her head in automatic denial. She wasn't

ready for this confrontation. Why hadn't she paid better attention to Dr. Rubin, or taken the time to go over the papers she'd been given?

Because she'd wanted some time to savor the news, to focus on the precious reality of being pregnant before having to face the future. Before having to face Jared Steele.

"You shouldn't have come."

"You should have called."

"I haven't had time to think!" She'd only wanted a week. She'd have called him tomorrow. "Go away."

"No."

"Then I'll call the police."

"And I'll call my lawyer."

No! Lisa's throat tightened with fear. That's exactly what she didn't want to happen. She didn't want a legal battle. Her heart hammered, and all her newly emerged motherly instincts shouted at her to run.

"Listen, if you don't want to be alone with me," he said, "we can drive to a restaurant. Believe me, you have nothing to fear. I won't hurt you." Though he tried to disguise his impatience, she saw it wasn't easy for him.

"I would hope not, I'm pregnant with your child."

Lisa straightened resolutely. What an odd statement to be making to a stranger. Yet her ingrained sense of honesty, which was as much a part of her as breathing, compelled her to admit he was right. They did need to talk. Hiding from the truth would accomplish nothing.

"We'll stay here," she decided. "I don't think this conversation is appropriate for a public restaurant."

She used her key to open the front door and led the way inside.

"Make yourself comfortable." She indicated the peach floral couch. Her hand shook slightly. For a moment she hesitated, uncertain about leaving him, but need overcame caution. "I'm going to take a moment to…ah, freshen up." Not waiting for a response, she turned and fled.

She desperately needed a moment alone.

She rushed into the bedroom, dropped her things and the teddy bear on the bed, then went to the dresser and pulled the envelope Dr. Rubin had given her from the bottom drawer. She stepped into the bathroom and locked the door.

She put the envelope on the vanity, ran cold water into the basin and splashed her hands and face. Feeling cooler, she perched on the edge of the tub and tore into the envelope. Quickly scanning the page inside, she was disappointed to find only a listing of Jared Steele's address and phone number.

Shoot, she'd expected more. She tried to recall her conversation with Dr. Rubin, in which they had discussed the mix-up.

The entire disastrous mishap revolved around the fact that she and Steele had been at the clinic at the same time. Another woman had been the scheduled recipient of Steele's specimen, but she'd canceled.

That's right, Lisa remembered, she'd had to change her original appointment due to an impromptu audit of the gallery books. What a horrible twist of fate. She'd been delighted to rearrange her appointment for the same day rather than having to wait an additional month.

According to Dr. Rubin, Mr. Steele had not intended his to be an anonymous donation. The doctor had apologized for the mix-up, assuring Lisa of her continued right to privacy.

Right. That didn't change the fact there was a man

in her living room. A man, she very much feared, who wanted to take her baby away from her.

How could he not want something so precious?

It hadn't been an easy decision to make. Artificial insemination. She had many doubts—from the beginning, when she first realized she was seriously contemplating such a controversial procedure, through the frank and personal interview she'd been subjected to at the clinic, and while she lay waiting in the sterile cubicle for the doctor to perform the procedure. The doubts, the fear, had been very strong at that point. Was she doing the right thing? For herself? For the baby? For the future?

Even after Dr. Rubin gave her the news, she'd panicked for a second as she realized there was no going back.

But ultimately? Yes, even with Jared Steele sitting in her living room, she knew she'd made the right decision. Her life would never be the same, but it would be changed for the better.

She had to believe that.

Once more, she glanced at the single page Dr. Rubin had given her. Another thing it didn't cover, and which she felt an urgent need to know, was how Steele came to be on her doorstep. Bending, she picked up the towel she'd dropped and draped it neatly over the railing. Then, summoning all her courage, she left the bathroom. The only way to find out what he knew and how he knew it was to ask him.

A group of paintings graced the wall inside Lisa's front door. The one in the center drew and held Jared's attention. It featured a little girl with honey-blond hair. The lone occupant of a small playground, she ignored the slides and swings other children would gleefully play upon. Instead, she stood before a crudely constructed easel. Jared clearly made out the rough form of a tree and beneath it little flowers. It was a painting pulsing with talent and steeped in emotions—loneliness, hope and determination were there for the viewer to see, to feel.

If what Jared knew of Lisa Langdon was true—and he had a fair idea it was, thanks to Zack's report—this picture more than belonged to Lisa. It *was* Lisa, a reminder of her childhood, a view of her isolated loneliness as an orphan and the promise of a dream-come-true all rolled into one.

The picture portrayed such innocence, such longing, he felt guilty for looking. He remembered her expression when she'd found him on her front porch, and he wished she hadn't looked so…threatened. He frowned and berated himself. The last thing he needed was to feel sympathy for her.

Lisa rounded the corner from the hall into her living room and came to an abrupt halt. Jared Steele stood with his gaze locked on *her* painting. She didn't care for the way he studied the picture. As if he could see beyond the surface scene into the heart of the artist. She felt vulnerable enough without him seeing into her soul.

When he suddenly turned and his piercing gaze came to rest on her, she changed her mind. She'd rather have him study the painting. Lifting her chin a notch, she stepped forward.

"How did you know where I live?" she demanded. Immediately she had his full, focused attention.

A sharp tingle ran down her spine. The man affected her, made her aware of him in ways she'd never experienced before. Was it terror or compassion she felt? She refused to think it might be attraction. Now wasn't the time to analyze her odd reaction, so she forced the sensation from her mind and onto the matter at hand.

He did not pretend to evade her question.

"Through your art." He indicated the pictures on the wall with a sweep of his hand. "Our conversation at the clinic was brief, but you mentioned you were an artist." He gave her a tense smile. "It's not every day a beautiful woman admires my nose."

"You happen to have a nice nose." Lisa self-consciously crossed her arms over her chest. She remembered the conversation he spoke of, she'd practically asked him to pose for her. Then, as now, the thought of him sprawled on display provoked a titillating image. A shiver of awareness rippled up her spine. "Anyway, I was speaking as an artist."

Dark eyebrows lifted over unblinking blue eyes, his gaze fixed on her face. The stare unnerved her. Though it took an effort, she forced herself to stand still. Not for anything would she show her uneasiness by fidgeting. Finally, he returned his attention to the picture.

"Whatever. You told me at the time that you'd given a piece of your work to Dr. Rubin." Slowly he swung to face her again. "I saw the painting."

Lisa nodded. She knew the picture well. She'd been struck by the doctor's strength, a strength tempered with gentleness and compassion. She'd done her best to put those traits into a portrait then given Dr. Rubin the painting as a gift.

"I was impressed." Jared continued his explanation. "It was also the only clue I had to your identity. You sign your work L. Langdon. A full name would have made finding you easier, but a last name was all I really needed."

Silence fell between them as Lisa absorbed this news. Her name was becoming recognizable in artistic circles, but she'd never had a show. Jared had done his homework, or more likely someone had done it for him. The result remained the same. He was here.

Here to take her child?

The bitter taste of fear coated her throat, and her calm facade shattered as the sensation of being cornered overcame all other emotions. "You should have given me more time."

"I tried. I intended to—"

"I have your name, address and telephone number."

"I know. I—"

"Dr. Rubin gave them to me. It was my decision whether I contacted you or not."

"That's not—"

"I would have called."

"I—"

"You should have given me more time."

"Enough."

Lisa shut her mouth with a soft plop. He was right. She'd begun to repeat herself. And her protests had no more impact now than they had earlier. Besides, what difference did it make *when* they had this discussion? She would never be ready.

"Do you know how I've felt?" he demanded, frustration thick in his voice. "This situation has preyed on my mind. I haven't been able to sleep, to eat. Damn, I can't even concentrate at work." He shook his dark head and seemed to consciously unclench his fists. "I've never allowed anything to interfere with my business."

The helplessness he'd obviously felt during those days echoed through his abrupt sentences, and Lisa fought a twinge of empathy. When he ran a tense hand over his hair, she turned away. Too well she understood his roiling emotions—uncertainty, relief, happiness, need and fear. She felt them all.

She moved to one of the chairs in the room and sank stiffly onto the edge of the seat. She needed to keep her feelings under strict control. Especially the fear.

"What are we going to do?" she asked with deliberate calm. She indicated for him to take a seat, but he didn't. He held his position and fixed her with a stare.

"Damned if I know."

The statement came from him, low and fierce. So low Lisa wondered if she'd heard right. "Excuse me?"

"Nothing." He moved to join her. "You understand what happened?" he asked, taking a seat across from her on the couch.

"Yes."

A sudden thought occurred to her. "Is this other woman pregnant by you too?"

"No." He considered her for a minute. "She canceled her appointment that day, and I haven't heard from her since."

Lisa remained tense, though deep inside her something eased.

"I want the child." The comment made his position clear and shattered her moment of peace.

She recoiled as if struck, devastated by the idea of giving up her baby. This was her worst fear realized. "You want the child?"

"Yes."

"No." She spoke softly, emphatically, a simple statement of fact. She would never hand over her child.

"That's it? No questions, no explanations, no discussions? Just no."

"That's it. I don't owe you any explanation, but I will tell you this." She sat forward, her eyes steady on his. She wanted to be sure he understood her every word. "I want this baby very much. For months I've planned this pregnancy. I've prepared myself in every way, mentally, physically, emotionally. You are a complication I didn't plan on."

She bowed her head. "When the doctor told me about the mix-up, everything changed. The knowledge became a dual-edged sword. I'm pregnant, a life is growing inside me. It's…awesome. But then there was you, a shadowy threat to me and my baby. It's not fair. To me this baby is everything. I can't give him or her up now, it's too late. I'd be giving up a part of myself."

After the impassioned speech, a heavy silence fell between them. For a tension-fraught moment their eyes remained locked together.

She watched for his reaction, but his expression revealed nothing. He understood, he was too intelligent not to, but understanding and acceptance were two different things.

He got up and began wandering around the room. His restlessness made her nervous. He was obviously a man of action, a man in control. This situation defied both. He stood staring at her painting again when he finally broke the taut silence.

"I was going to give the other woman fifty thousand dollars at conception and another fifty thousand upon the baby's birth. I'm willing to offer you the same arrangement."

Lisa shook her head at his arrogance. He hadn't listened to a word she'd said.

Anger brewed deep inside her. With quiet dignity, she rose and moved to the door. Holding it open, she looked him in the eye. "Please leave."

Irritation flared in his blue eyes before he hooded his gaze, hiding the displeasure. "We need to discuss this—"

"I have nothing further to say. My child is not for sale!"

Wind whipped through the open window of Lisa's Nissan as she raced down Highway 8, then north on Highway 5. She breathed deeply of the cleansing sea air, welcoming the rush of wind over her face and through her hair.

She was running. Fast and far. And scared.

Jared Steele wanted *her* baby.

He couldn't have it—him—her. Not now. Not ever. Her breath hitched on a smothered sob. Ten minutes after he'd left her house, she'd followed him out the door. She'd needed to get away, put time and miles between her and the threat against her child.

This baby was her family, her blood, her future. Already she loved, already she felt a connection, a bonding. She had plans...

And they didn't include Jared Steele.

What made him think he could buy—buy!—her precious babe? How dare he ask that of her? Who did he think he was?

The baby's father. The barrage of internal questions all had the same devastating answer. *He was the baby's father.*

She wondered what circumstances in a man's life led him to hire a woman to have his child, then decided she didn't want to know.

As the hours and the miles flew by, Lisa slowly came to grips with her panic. She finally calmed down enough to remember she'd never planned to have her baby at anyone else's expense, physically or emotionally. By using artificial insemination, the baby would be hers and hers alone.

But that's not what happened.

The mix-up that had brought Jared Steele into her life was no more his fault than hers. She struggled to gain a sense of fairness, to remember that she shouldn't hold someone else's mistake against him.

Lisa pulled into a hotel parking lot just as the sun sank into the ocean off the coast of Santa Barbara. Deep streaks of pink, orange and magenta burst across the sky in a magnificent sunset. Drawn by memories of her childhood, she detoured past the hotel office and walked across the grass to the sand.

Her parents used to bring her to the beach late in the day. Before the sun went down, they'd roast wieners and marshmallows then walk barefoot in the waves. After dark, Daddy would feed the fire and tell stories, wonderful pictures painted with words. Lisa would climb into his lap and fall asleep to the sound of his voice.

Now she sat alone and watched the sky turn slowly purple then black.

She sat, and she watched, and she remembered.

And when she left the beach for the hotel, she knew she'd be driving south in the morning. Not because of what was fair or right, or because of Steele's feelings.

She was going home because of her dad. Because the best gift she could give her child was a father.

On Saturday, a week and a half after she learned she was pregnant and two days after her impulsive trip up the coast, Lisa took Ashley to lunch to fill her in on everything that had happened. "One hundred thousand dollars?" Ashley disturbed more than one guest at nearby tables with her startled exclamation. "What kind of animal tries to buy a woman's baby? There ought to be a law against that type of thing."

Lisa glanced around, conscious of the delicacy of

their conversation. She needn't have worried. The subdued atmosphere of the Coral Room had already soothed the other diners into returning to their meals.

"That was my reaction, too. But more along the lines of what makes a man hire a woman to have his child?"

"He's ugly as sin?"

Blood rushed into Lisa's cheeks. How she wished she could confirm Ashley's guess. She still smarted when she remembered her awareness of him.

Ashley, of course, immediately read her reaction. She arched a dark eyebrow at Lisa. "Not ugly, huh?"

Lisa shook her head. "Gorgeous."

"Hmm. It must be a mental defect then."

A warm rush of love swelled through her. She reached over and squeezed Ashley's hand. "You are priceless. Thanks for the unwavering support. Obviously he's missing something in his life. It's sad really."

Ashley sent her a sharp glance. "Stop it this instant, Lisa Langdon. You are, without a doubt, the most empathetic, caring person I know, but not even you can condone this Steele character's proposition."

"Of course not. I'd never consider his offer. And I'm not defending him, but—"

"No buts. Listen to yourself, Lisa. Don't you have any sense of self-preservation at all?"

"Yes, I do. You know I do."

Lisa looked into her friend's anxious features. She knew Ashley would never be able to understand. They were too alike in some ways and too different in others. Ashley, with her flaming red hair and a figure that embodied the term *built,* led a vivacious life. Her emotions were close to the surface, anger, joy, concern, passion—rarely was Ashley calm. But like Lisa, Ashley had a well of deeper emotions she kept hidden. The years in foster care had taught both of them to protect their inner selves.

"Yeah, I know." Concern etched a frown above Ashley's intelligent brown eyes. She reached across the table and placed her hand over Lisa's. "I think you should talk to a lawyer."

Lisa cringed and shook her head. She'd chosen to use a clinic and artificial insemination to avoid ever having a legal issue raised regarding parentage or custody.

The thought of drawing public attention sent a raw wave of panic through her, making her sick to her stomach. She associated the feelings with the days after her parents died in the accident.

For twelve hours she'd been stuck in the crushed car—watched as her parents slowly died before her eyes. She'd been ten and alone. After the rescue, officials and judges had all spoken to her, but mostly around her. And there'd been the media making everything public, the details of her life bandied about as everyone waited to hear what became of the poor little orphaned girl.

All she'd known was that her parents were dead, and the grown-ups were talking about things she didn't understand. Then she'd gone to live with strangers. And the loneliness began. Until she met Ashley.

Ashley ignored her negative response. "Let me call my lawyer. I'll set up an appointment for tomorrow—"

"No." Lisa couldn't consider that option, not yet. She'd decided to acknowledge Jared for her child's sake. She hoped they'd be able to work something out without going through the courts.

"At least think about it. What if he sues for custody?"

The mere thought sickened Lisa. Mentally, she compared her impressions of Jared Steele past and present. She'd seen a different side of him a month ago when she first met him at the clinic, charming rather than intense, concerned rather than demanding.

He possessed a self-confidence, a sureness of self that did not demand procreation as proof of his mature virility. His controlled movements portrayed him as a man of authority, a man in command of those around him. Those characteristics held as true today as they had a month ago. He wanted a child so he'd acted on that feeling in a direct and honest manner.

How could she condemn him for that? Hadn't she done the same thing herself? Hadn't she chosen the same method as he to achieve the same goal.

"He hasn't threatened to fight me for custody," she answered Ashley's challenge. "Somehow I don't think he will. If we can settle this between us without involving lawyers and the press, I'd prefer to do so."

"Why won't you protect yourself?" Ashley fought Lisa's stubbornness with persistence.

"If I were to speak to a lawyer now, I'd feel as if I was asking for trouble. You know it's never been my intention to have my happiness, my baby, at anyone else's expense."

Ashley sighed and sat back in her chair. "True. If you'd taken my advice, none of this would have happened."

"No, there'd be a different set of problems. The whole point of using artificial insemination was to avoid this kind of hassle."

Ashley shrugged as if to say maybe, maybe not. She redeemed herself with a sincerely stated, "I'm here if you need me."

"I know." Lisa said, smiling her gratitude. "I promise to think about talking to a lawyer. Now, enough of this topic. I need something else to occupy my mind. You said you had a check for me?"

"I do, minus my commission. I almost feel guilty taking the money. Your stuff practically sells itself."

Lisa inclined her head. "You don't feel guilty when you collect your commission on the sale of a house, this is no different."

"It is different, that's business. This is a hobby and my pleasure."

A top-selling real estate agent in the San Diego area, Ashley's first love was art. She majored in it in college. So when Lisa needed an agent for her art and Ashley volunteered on a trial basis, Lisa happily accepted Ashley's offer. Lisa had been more than satisfied with the results. Mrs. Dumond only knew of Ashley's work in real estate, but she had been impressed.

"The same could be said of my painting. Another sale. That's three this month."

"You're hot, my friend. Now listen, I think it's time to show Mrs. Dumond some of your work," Ashley said, mentioning the manager of the Shore Side Gallery.

"I don't know, Ashley. I've explained how I feel about approaching her. I work at the gallery, I'd feel as if I were putting her on the spot."

"How can you think that?" Ashley signaled the waitress to bring their bill. "You're a rising new talent in this area. Your name is becoming known. I'm surprised she hasn't asked to see a few pieces of her own accord."

"Well, she did bring up the subject the other day." Reluctantly, Lisa imparted the news.

"What? And you didn't tell me? What was said? Don't leave out a single detail."

"She'd heard you were representing me and was, of course, impressed."

"Of course." Ashley didn't believe in false modesty. "But what did she say about you?"

"It was a brief conversation, the 'what have you been doing lately' kind of chitchat. She made a vague suggestion to bring in a few pieces for her to see."

"I knew it! And you wouldn't have told me if I hadn't dragged it out of you."

"I don't want to take advantage." Lisa watched Ashley sign the receipt in her flowing script and then they rose to leave.

"You don't want to be rejected, you mean. Well, you needn't worry, kid, she's going to love your style. And it's not taking advantage. We're offering her the opportunity to promote an exceptional talent."

Lisa pulled the other woman close for a one-armed hug. "What would I do without you? I love to paint, but sometimes I wonder if the world thinks I'm wasting my time. Just when I'm feeling my lowest, you always come through for me."

"This world would be a sorry place if it weren't for the brightness and color you bring to it." Ashley returned her hug with an arm around Lisa's waist. "Now, enough of the sentimental. I'm going to be late for my next appointment. I'll be by on Thursday to help pick out the pieces to show Dumond. Don't forget to put in an appearance at the Pavilion Gallery. It's good for business. They like to tell the tourists they know the artist."

Ashley rattled off a few more orders as she walked a few steps backward, already separating herself from Lisa. The last was said with a wink and a wave, then she turned and picked up her pace. Lisa knew her thoughts were already on another client.

In this she was wrong. Ashley stopped a short distance away to turn back and advise, "Forget about Steele, he's a jerk!"

Lisa watched her friend climb into her car and drive away. "Yeah," she muttered, "that's easy for you to say."

But she was determined to give it a try. Sea World beckoned from across the bay. She'd drive over and spend the day there. The exercise would do her good. She also wanted to be surrounded with children, in celebration of her condition. This child, growing within her, was very important to her. He or she would receive all the love Lisa longed to give.

For the rest of the afternoon, she wandered through the amusement park, absorbing the sun and observing the people. Tired out, she settled down beside a tide pool and peered into the shallow depths.

The sea creatures, usually so colorful and interesting, were obscured by the glare of the late-afternoon sun. Instead, she encountered a mirror-like image of herself. She gazed at her reflection, fascinated by the sudden thought of what her child might look like. Would the baby have her delicate bone structure and fair coloring?

She closed her eyes and tried to picture a miniature version of herself with golden hair and golden eyes. The image refused to form. Instead, her imagination conjured up a tiny being with dark curls, sapphire eyes and a perfect little nose.

Her eyes sprang open in shock. Those were traitorous thoughts. Then she caught herself. She'd love her child regardless of his or her physical attributes. At least now, if the baby had dark hair and blue eyes, she'd know where the coloring came from.

Chapter Three

"Jared, the messenger from Confidential Carriers is here to pick up the package you want delivered."

"Thank you, Martha, send him in."

As he disconnected the interoffice call, Jared reached to retrieve the envelope containing the check for Lisa Langdon. The legal-size package also carried an iron-clad contract relieving Miss Langdon of all rights and obligations toward his child. He hoped once she saw the money, she'd take the deal.

It felt wrong, even as he handed the envelope to the young man and watched him leave the room. It just felt wrong.

He couldn't allow himself to care. Twelve years ago he'd made the wrong decision. He'd misjudged a woman and she'd aborted their unborn child. Every instinct he possessed urged him to get control of this situation, and if that meant buying his way out, he'd do it.

The image of Dr. Clarice Rubin lecturing him on his involvement with his child came to him. "How can you feel connected to your child if you aren't there to feel the first movements within the womb, to feel those flutterings grow stronger, to be there at the birth and see your child make its entrance into the world? The very distance you require from the mother will also apply to the child."

Jared refused to admit that Dr. Rubin's comments had touched him. He fought to put her arguments out of his mind. He knew his motives for wanting a child were selfish.

For years he'd lived with the guilt of the past. With the birth of this baby, he hoped to fill the emptiness he'd carried inside for so long.

He craved peace.

From the past. And into the future. The peace to run his life without being pressured to marry and start a family. He wanted to be able to visit his family without being attacked by some husband-hungry female aiding his mother in her campaign to end his single status.

The reason he'd avoided having a child up to now was simple. After the betrayal he'd suffered while in college, he'd never let another woman close enough emotionally to risk giving her a baby.

Which brought him back to Lisa Langdon. Lovely, warm, gentle, he found her independence and inner strength intensely frustrating. And damn arousing. Restlessly, he shifted in his chair, uncomfortable with his thoughts.

How open she'd been at the clinic. She'd made no excuses for staring boldly; she'd simply stated why. A reluctant smile tugged up the corners of his mouth. He would never have guessed his nose might be the first of his features to attract a woman. Many raved about his eyes, his baby blues, and an equal number admired his hair, wanting to run their fingers through the dark waves. A brazen few had made no secret that they craved his body.

But not Lisa Langdon. She liked his nose. Unbelievable. No telling where the conversation might have gone if the nurse hadn't disturbed them.

Immediately, he suppressed the notion. She was carrying his child. He couldn't afford sexual thoughts about her.

The situation called for positive action, which he'd taken. By sending the contract, he regained control yet maintained the personal distance he deemed necessary.

He lifted the telephone receiver and punched in his personal assistant's extension.

"Yes, sir?"

"Martha, I'm expecting a call from Lisa Langdon. Put it through. If I'm not in my office, find me."

"How about this one?" In the studio, Lisa turned the canvas she held to face Ashley. The beach scene glowed with the vibrant colors of sunset. A sand castle resided just out of reach of the incoming tide. Simple in design, the castle had obviously been the efforts of a young child, evidenced by the abandoned toy bucket and shovel half buried in the sand. In the distance a family walked along the shore.

"Yeah, I like that one. Let me put it with the others."

Lisa straightened. They'd been sorting through the paintings in her studio for the past hour, deciding on which to show to Mrs. Dumond. "I think three is enough, don't you?" Hands at the small of her back, she arched backward to relieve the strain of being bent over.

"For Dumond?" Ashley answered in a distracted tone. "Yes, I think so. I just want to see what else you have here." She continued to flip from canvas to canvas, stopping to study each one.

Lisa watched Ashley for a minute, but the unnerving experience of seeing her work scrutinized and assessed, not for the beauty of the scene, but for its sales potential became too much to take. Being present was a necessary evil, certainly, but one an artist should avoid whenever possible for her own peace of mind. Even knowing the appraiser was her best friend didn't help.

"I'll get us something cold to drink."

A knock on the front door stopped her on the way to the kitchen. The detour left her holding a legal-size envelope. She flipped it front to back but found no return address. Mystified, she tore open the package and extracted the contents—a contract and another envelope with her name across the front.

"What...?"

After reading the first few paragraphs on the contract, her blood began to simmer. As she read on, her anger grew in proportion to the absolute audacity of Jared Steele.

"How dare he—"

The legal document, all three pages of it, covered every contingency required to sever her link with her baby. Jared expected her to have the child then hand the baby over and completely disassociate herself from their lives.

"What gives him the right—"

That he'd had the utter gall to have such a contract drawn up went beyond her comprehension. She couldn't believe it, yet she held the proof in her hands.

"Who are you talking to?" Ashley joined Lisa in the living room.

"Huh?" Lisa swung around at the question, only then realizing she'd been speaking her disjointed thoughts aloud. "Look at this." She thrust the papers into her friend's hands.

"What is it?"

"Read it. You're used to contracts, you tell me." Lisa paced while Ashley quickly scanned the official document.

"My goodness." Ashley didn't lift her eyes from reading. "The jerk is serious."

"Who does he think he is?" Unconsciously, Lisa rubbed her arms in a defensive, frustrated manner.

"What's this?" Ashley held up the second envelope with Lisa's name on it.

Lisa's frown deepened. "I don't know. I haven't opened it yet." With little enthusiasm, she accepted the proffered envelope. What more could he have sent? It wouldn't be good news, of that she was sure.

The rush of fury she felt upon spying the check was expected, the sense of betrayal was not. She extended the check for Ashley to see.

"Three hundred thousand dollars." Ashley whistled under her breath. "Unsigned, of course. Your signature in exchange for his. The man's got nerve." Concern showed in her brown eyes when she lifted her gaze. "And bucks. Are you going to be able to fight him?"

"If it takes everything I have." Lisa voiced each word with firm conviction. She inhaled a deep, calming breath. Carefully, she fitted the check and contract back into the envelope. "Can you give me a ride down to Jared's office in Mission Valley? I'm too upset to drive right now."

"Don't you think you should wait? Give yourself a chance to calm down."

"This isn't the kind of thing it helps to brood about."

"Okay. If you're sure." Ashley's tone revealed her doubts. "Maybe you should call the attorney now."

Lisa nodded. "You're right. But I want to talk to Jared Steele first."

"I'm not sure that's a good idea."

"Please. This is between me and him. I'm not going to let him think he can buy me."

Ashley relented. "Let me get my purse from the studio."

"Thank you, Ashe," Lisa said gravely twenty minutes later when they pulled to a stop in front of a twelve-story glass and steel building. A sign labeled their destination as the Steele Inc. complex. "Don't worry. I'm simply going to return these items and try, once again, to get it through the man's thick skull that my baby isn't for sale. No matter how many carrots he dangles."

"Carrots? Are you sure you want to do this? You're not making sense. I'd be happy to drive you home." Real worry shadowed Ashley's stunning features.

"Carrots. You know, as in a carrot dangled in front of a horse in order to get it to go where you want. Well, I'm not a horse, and no amount of carrots are going to sway me." She stepped from the car and closed the door. "Thanks for the ride. Please don't wait. I'll find my own way home."

As she walked determinedly into the building, she tried to plan her strategy, but it wasn't in her to be premeditated about this. Her emotions were too raw to plan ahead as she usually liked to do. She'd have to rely on her instincts, jumbled as they were, to guide her through the coming meeting.

She bypassed reception on the main floor to step directly into the elevator. An unsteady finger pressed the button for the top floor. Something told her Jared would situate his office at the supreme point of power, at the top.

The elevator stopped at several floors, people came and went. Lisa rested against the cushioned panel in the back, where she tried to control her breathing in an effort to calm her pounding heart.

A soft *ping* announced her arrival, and the doors swished open to another large reception area. The decor consisted of white contemporary furniture, lush green plants and a wall of glass. Royal blue carpeting, deep and plush, absorbed the sound of her steps. Modern prints containing complementing blues and golds brightened the walls.

Lisa met her first obstacle in the blond, beautiful, coolly chic receptionist. Boldly, Lisa approached the desk and stated her purpose. "I'm here to see Jared Steele."

"Do you have an appointment?" The woman's quick, assessing glance, taking in Lisa's casual slacks and cotton blouse, indicated doubt.

Lisa lifted her chin to a proud angle. "He'll see me."

"Mr. Steele is unavailable. Would you care to make an appointment for next week? Perhaps one of the executives could help you?"

In the normal course of events, the superior tone and icy disposition would have been intimidating. Today, Lisa was in no mood to put up with condescension.

"I'll wait."

"It'll be a waste of time. Mr. Steele doesn't see anyone without an appointment."

Lisa narrowed her eyes, annoyed. Enough was definitely enough. She wouldn't be patronized. Nor would she be ignored.

"He'll see me," she repeated. Not waiting for a response, she made for an unmarked door located behind the receptionist's desk, the woman hot on her heels. Mr. Unavailable probably sat at his desk at this very minute, masterminding some new plot to wrestle her child away from her. Well, it wouldn't happen, and the sooner she let him know it, the better.

The door opened into an office, but it wasn't Jared Steele who stood at her abrupt entrance. A mature woman faced her. Though in her middle years, the woman in no way resembled the motherly type. Instead, she portrayed starched efficiency.

Lisa hesitated just inside the door. Should she advance or retreat? She had no real choice in the matter. The importance of her mission prevented any form of withdrawal. She marched over to confront what she hoped would be the final obstacle in reaching her objective.

"I'm here to see Jared Steele."

"Mr. Steele is in a conference. Did you have an appointment?" the woman asked, polite but distant. The question seemed aimed more at the receptionist who had followed Lisa into the room than at Lisa.

"I tried to explain to her that Mr. Steele doesn't see

visitors,'' the receptionist said, "but she pushed by me anyway.''

The older woman nodded, acknowledging the explanation, then addressed Lisa. "I'm sorry, but Sandra is correct, and Mr. Steele's meeting is expected to last several hours. Perhaps you'd care to arrange a time for next week?''

Lisa began to wonder if Jared had left orders to waylay her if she came by. But that didn't make sense. She'd think he'd be waiting to hear from her.

"I'm not waiting until next week. Appointment or no appointment, I'm not leaving here until I've seen him.''

With a muffled reference to security, the receptionist backed from the room.

The secretary came around her desk. "I'm sure you don't wish to cause trouble. If you insist on seeing Mr. Steele, I believe he's free next Friday at two.''

Lisa stared at the woman. The prospect of holding in her feelings for a whole week spurred her to action. "I'll wait here.'' She turned to seek a seat.

"Miss, I really must object. Sandra is calling security. Mr. Steele is a very busy man, it's imperative he stick to a schedule. Now, if you'll give me your name, I'll set you up for next Friday.''

Lisa, her dignity intact, sank into a white modular chair near the window. "My name is Lisa Langdon, and I'm staying.''

The older woman's eyes widened slightly, her cool demeanor cracking at the mention of Lisa's name. She quickly composed herself. "You should have given your name sooner.'' She spoke the reprimand around a brittle smile. "Please excuse me, I'll see if Mr. Steele can be disturbed.''

After his secretary left the room, Lisa sagged in relief. Scenes were not her forte. Then she straightened again and squared her shoulders. The fight had only just begun.

Hard on the heels of the secretary's disappearance came the reappearance of Sandra, the receptionist. A man shadowed her. He was tall, broad and muscular, a mass of sheer masculinity. His features were expressionless except for watchful black eyes. He knew of her presence as soon as he stepped across the threshold. Sandra was slower in noticing her new position.

"Martha, Farrell's here. Martha?" She walked deeper into the room in her search for the other woman, heading for yet another door.

"She's gone to find Mr. Steele," Lisa volunteered.

"What...?" Startled, Sandra spun around to face Lisa. She appeared disconcerted to find Lisa sitting by the window. "You're still here."

"I'm waiting to see Mr. Steele."

The blonde's eyes shifted from Lisa to the man named Farrell in a significant gesture. But before any further action could be instigated, Martha returned.

"Sandra, you may return to your desk. Zack, I'm sorry you were disturbed. Everything is under control. Jared will be here in a few minutes to speak with Miss Langdon." She turned to Lisa. "He asked me to have you wait in his office."

Lisa rose on shaky legs to precede Martha into the next room. The decor surprised her. The two previous rooms had been designed to project stark productivity—business, pure and simple. This room suggested comfort. Large, high-backed chairs invited occupation, a well-stocked bar lent an air of informality, and an intimate conversational grouping of two chairs and a sofa hinted that not all negotiations were conducted over the imposing length of the mahogany desk.

The colors were reversed in here: white carpeting and royal blue furnishing with subtle, deeper touches of gold. Steele enjoyed the benefit of a corner office. Lisa crossed the wide expanse of the room, drawn once again, as she had been in the outer office, to the large picture window.

The panoramic view of Mission Valley was spectacular. The historical sight of Mission San Diego de Alcala wasn't visible from where she stood, but the lush, green vegetation and concrete jungle of the rest of the valley spread before her, interrupted occasionally by the ribbons of freeways. At any other time, the artist in her would have itched to capture the contrasting beauty of the scene, but not today.

"Miss Langdon."

Lisa closed her eyes against the view. He was here. The waiting was over. Slowly, she faced him. Jared leaned against the closed door of his office. Their gazes met and held across the space separating them. She held his probing stare for a full minute, then lowered her lashes and pulled from her purse the dreaded envelope.

Without a word, she walked to his desk and emptied the thousands of tiny pieces on his leather blotter.

Jared eyed the mess. "We have to talk."

She remained silent, watching him, not answering until he'd circled the room and come to a stop on the far side of his desk.

"I think that states my position quite clearly." Lisa indicated the pile of paper littering the desktop.

"We both know it doesn't."

"I won't sign away my rights to my child for any

amount of money.'' Passion breathed life into each word. Again she grasped for control, couldn't quite find it. ''So,'' she challenged, ''where does that leave us?''

''Back at square one, I'd say.'' Jared moved to hold the back of his chair. With the sweep of a lean hand, he invited her to take a seat.

She complied, less for comfort than because she doubted the shaky ability of her knees to hold her up much longer. She would, however, have preferred for Jared to join her in the companion chair rather than perch above her on the edge of his desk.

A sudden question occurred to Lisa. ''Are you married?''

''What?'' Jared glared at her, unprepared for the change in subject.

''I asked, are you married? I think it's a valid question. Is it because your wife is unable to conceive that you went to the clinic?''

Jared arched an eyebrow at her. ''It's none of your business.'' His tone turned bitter. ''You were content enough not knowing the father's background when you decided to have the child artificially.''

''That was before he showed up on my doorstep.'' Not even by the flicker of an eyelash did Lisa let on how the harsh statement hurt.

He considered her. ''Would it make a difference?''

''No,'' she assured him. ''It would just add another complication to an already complicated issue.''

''Well, I'm not married.''

Jared leaned back, his arms crossed over his chest, and surveyed Lisa, assessing her.

''I am, however, in a position to ensure my child never wants for anything.''

She reacted like a wildcat.

"What's that supposed to mean?" She flew forward in her chair, fire swirling like molten gold in her eyes. "I may not have the wealth you obviously do, but I'm well able to support my child. And I don't believe you can provide everything. I have yet to hear you mention the word *love* in connection with the baby."

Too furious to sit still a moment longer, she rose to stand stiffly, her back to him. How dare he suggest she lacked the ability to provide for her child?

"I care about the baby, damn it, but that's not the point. You say you didn't plan on me, well, lady, the feeling is mutual. You have something of mine, and I want it back!" Jared asserted.

Lisa paled and sank back into her chair. A stricken look dulled the golden shine of her eyes.

"Look, I'm sorry. I didn't mean to insult you. It's just…this pregnancy thing." He shook his head and avoided her soulful gaze. "I'm not in control, and I don't know…how to handle it."

Lisa listened to his stilted confession and felt a surprising sympathy for him. Silently, she cursed herself for a fool. She needed to focus on self-preservation, but she couldn't be selfish in the face of his need. She cared. Not enough to consider giving up her baby, but enough perhaps to compromise. Maybe.

She felt a strong link with this man that went beyond the fact she carried his seed. Though every time she remembered that intimate detail, a warmth spread through her whole being. She'd like to deny that the father's presence made a difference, but honesty prevented her from doing so. In many ways, her pregnancy had become more real after she'd met Jared Steele.

Angry as he sometimes made her, she couldn't deny her own nature. An empathetic soul, she too easily saw things from his perspective. What if he were the one nurturing their child inside his body? Hardly humanly possible, but the ridiculous notion reminded her she'd feel as helpless in that eventuality as he did now.

"You're right, Mr. Steele—"

"Jared, damn it, call me Jared."

Lisa jumped, startled by his unexpected outburst. After his confession, he couldn't seem to reestablish his cool, impersonal approach. She barely kept her mouth from dropping open when he unbent enough to run his hand along the back of his neck in a stress-easing gesture. He looked at her and away again quickly, not quite meeting her eyes.

Jared Steele was human, after all.

He dropped into the chair next to hers, yet Lisa couldn't bring herself to break the silence. He was close, too close for her to avoid being distracted by his male attractiveness, much more obvious in his vulnerable state. She made a move to rise. "I should leave."

A strong, tanned hand settled on her smaller one, holding her still, forcing her to face him.

"Please stay," he requested, releasing his grip on her slender fingers when she eased back into her seat. "We need to work this out."

"The only answer is shared custody," she said.

A deep scowl creased his forehead as he contemplated her proposal somewhat suspiciously. "How do you suggest we do this 'sharing'?" Bitterness returned to distort his deep voice. "I suppose you'll want financial compensation for the time you're willing to give the baby over to me."

Lisa inhaled a bracing breath, as stunned as he by her generous suggestion. She couldn't say where the thought had come from, but the response he'd given wasn't promising.

She reached out and grasped his arm. Under her fingers lay the hard strength of his muscular forearm. He'd shifted his attention away from her while uttering his last comment, almost as if he knew better, but couldn't prevent the words.

"You don't know me," she said. "We don't know each other. Obviously something happened in your past to make you bitter. That's none of my business, but don't you think there are enough pitfalls in this situation without adding undue prejudice?"

She slid her hand along his arm in an unconscious caress, pulling her hand away when she realized what she was doing.

"Listen to us," she said. "The baby isn't even born, and we're already arguing over visits and finances. I don't want that. My child's life is going to be full of love, laughter and happiness, not cold arguments and quiet discord."

The baby's welfare came first for her, she hoped he understood the importance of that.

Jared greeted her declaration in silence. "You're right," he consented. "Perhaps we should shelve the discussions regarding visitation rights, finances and general responsibility until we've had a chance to get to know each other better. Why don't we start now? I'll give you a tour of the place."

Relieved by his ready cooperation, Lisa relaxed the control she'd been exerting over herself. "I'd like that."

Suddenly, with the lessening of the tension, she fought a losing battle against a storm of tears. Distressed and embarrassed, she pushed to her feet. Mumbling, "I'm sorry," she turned away, trying to hide her tears.

"Lisa?" Jared followed her. Solicitously, he cupped the curve of her shoulders in the palms of his hands.

She tensed at the light pressure. "I'm f-fine." Her voice broke despite her efforts to appear calm. "Just give me a minute."

Lisa snuffed and shuddered. She was embarrassed by the waterworks, not prone to crying at a moment's notice. Jared's understanding helped. His closeness warmed her even after the unexpected tears disappeared.

She dipped her head to hide a smile. She had the strangest desire to laugh out loud at some of the things he whispered in an attempt to comfort her. He'd just recited Humpty Dumpty. His grasp tightened at her renewed shaking, and she guiltily managed to control her mirth.

Poor Jared, he'd obviously let himself in for more than he'd anticipated. Clearly, this whole thing was new to him. She moved away from his hold. With a sniff, she accepted the handkerchief he offered.

"I'm sorry," she said into the starched cloth.

Jared brushed aside her apology. "It's all right. I've been doing some reading on the subject. It's not uncommon for a pregnant woman to cry for no apparent reason." He stepped back, his hands thrust into his pants pockets. "You okay now?"

Lisa nodded. He'd floored her again, though she tried to hide her reaction. She wanted to be able to dismiss him as the lowest of the low. After all, he'd tried to buy her baby. Then he threw her off balance by expressing genuine concern. His interest in something as mundane as the crying habits of pregnant women indicated a level of involvement on his part that went beyond the surface desire to produce a child.

And that scared her.

She'd agreed to a truce, and she meant to do her best to keep the peace. But she couldn't help the over-whelming sensation of fear that washed over her. He was committed to his child. *Her* child.

Would she be able to hold her own against him?

Chapter Four

Lisa enjoyed sharing in Jared's enthusiasm for his work. Every word out of his mouth expressed his love and dedication for his business.

"At Steele Inc., we don't just design and build a building, we undertake a project from beginning to end. We have more than twenty offices worldwide. Our employees are experts in engineering, drafting, interior design, landscaping and many other related professions." Pride sounded in Jared's voice.

"Twenty offices?" she asked, impressed, overwhelmed. They'd woven in and out of every corner of Steele Inc. Maintenance must be the only department they hadn't visited. A corporation of this size took power and capital to maintain. If he decided to fight her for custody, the wealth and resources he had at his disposal would be awesome.

"Most are satellite branches. The main offices are in

London, New York, Hong Kong and here in San Diego.''

"Excuse me, Jared, may I have a moment?" A portly man with thinning brown hair stopped beside Jared. The man held a stack of files in his arms.

"Richard." Jared greeted the man and introduced Lisa. It surprised her how familiar he was with all his employees, how easily he greeted each by name. From mail clerks to vice presidents, he never once stumbled over a name. Yet he retained total authority over everyone and everything. He hesitated now, as if about to deny the man the time he requested.

"Go ahead, Jared. I don't mind waiting," she urged, ready for a break.

"I'll only be a minute. Richard?" Jared accepted the papers the man handed him.

Lisa spied a chair a short distance away and gratefully made her way to it. She welcomed the chance to sit.

"I'll take care of it, Jared," Richard said. "Sorry to have disturbed you." The executive shuffled the handful of papers and made his way down the hall.

Jared swung around to rejoin Lisa, eager to continue with the tour. Surprisingly, he enjoyed showing her around, telling her about the family business. It had been some time since he'd personally escorted a guest on a tour. He should do so more often.

"Lisa...where?" he questioned under his breath. He scanned the area, stopping when his gaze lit upon Lisa's sleeping figure curled into one of the visitor chairs. Immediately, the momentary tension seeped away. Something softened inside him at the sight of the beautiful woman seated a few feet away, her head pillowed on a closed fist.

Woman? She looked more like a child.

Another wave of tenderness washed over him. Because he didn't trust the emotion, he cautioned himself against giving in to the feeling. At this moment she may have the appearance of an innocent waif, but he mustn't forget she was a woman, a woman pregnant with his child.

He reminded himself of this even as he moved forward and carefully swung her into his arms. His gut tightened when he looked upon the translucent complexion of the woman cradled in his arms.

No doubt about it, she was going to be a danger to his peaceful existence.

He'd finally begun to recognize some of the feelings he'd found so unsettling during the past few days.

There were the protective instincts, of course, but today he had unraveled another emotion. A newness, or freshness, or just the sense of being alive again. His awareness for the world around him intensified when he was with her. He saw things through new eyes, an artist's eyes, her eyes.

Today, for example. As Lisa asked questions and showed interest in his life's work, he'd known a renewed pleasure in the everyday aspects of his business.

In none of his relationships with other women had he experienced this elemental sense of self and of selflessness. The women he'd known in the past had been self-absorbed, his relationships with them shallow. He'd purposely fostered the "no ties" element.

Ignoring raised eyebrows and dropping mouths, he carried Lisa down corridors and across rooms, stopping only once when he ran into his chief of security. Zack Farrell came out of the elevator as Jared prepared to step inside.

"Zack." Jared nodded to the man who held open the doors, then he stepped forward, maneuvering his sleeping passenger into the limited space.

"Quite a handful you have there," Zack responded.

"Yeah," Jared acknowledged, but said nothing more.

"In more ways than one. She wouldn't have given up easily this morning. I'm glad you decided to see her."

"Caused a little commotion, did she?"

"Let's just say she's a very determined young woman." Zack removed his hand and the doors slid closed.

In his office, Jared settled Lisa carefully upon the couch. Why hadn't she told him she was getting tired? Why hadn't he seen her weariness for himself? Shrugging out of his jacket, he tucked the garment securely around her then left her to sleep in peace.

At his desk, he sat and pulled open the top left-hand drawer. On top was a book he'd been reading by a well-known obstetrician entitled *A Father's Guide to Prenatal Survival*. A corny title, but nonetheless an excellent source of information.

He read while Lisa rested. Every so often he glanced up to watch her sleep. She'd exhausted herself today. Of course, this was all new to her. She probably wasn't used to tiring so easily. Or so the book said. The author also entreated him, as the father, to show patience and understanding when the expectant mother encountered new limitations to her endurance.

He would have to keep a better eye on her.

Dr. Rubin's lecture sprung to mind once more. She'd cautioned him about the distance he'd feel if he kept himself isolated from his child's mother. The opposite had happened, which was what she'd really meant all along. The better he got to know Lisa, the closer he felt to his child.

Lisa stirred, snuggling deeper into the cushions. Something had disturbed her. Opening one eye, she investigated her surroundings and found them to be vaguely familiar. Her lid fluttered down again. Sleepily, she searched her memory for the events leading to this comfortable couch.

Oh yes, Jared, an argument, tears, a truce, the tour, a chair. She must have fallen asleep in the chair, which didn't explain how she'd ended up on Jared's office couch. Surely he hadn't carried her through the building?

Where was he, anyway? And what had interrupted her sleep? She drifted, halfway between wakefulness and renewed slumber, letting the happenings of the day catch up with her.

Another sound disturbed her. Dragging her eye open with the same reluctance as before, Lisa sought the source.

Jared.

She watched as he came into the room then closed her eyes again. The click of the door must have aroused her when he left the room.

The cushion beside her depressed with his weight. She gathered the strength to open both eyes. He didn't smile, but for the first time gentleness softened his expression.

Jared brushed a honey-toned strand of hair from her face. Dewy-eyed, her cheeks flushed from sleep, she looked utterly feminine. "Did you have a nice nap?"

She nodded.

"You should have let me know when you got tired."

"I know." She winced self-consciously. "I was fine. The fatigue just sort of knocked me out."

"Sudden exhaustion is a symptom of early pregnancy. You'll have to make sure you get a full night's sleep every night and be prepared to rest each day."

"Uh-oh." Lisa groaned. "You've been reading again. A little knowledge is a dangerous thing, you know."

It never occurred to Jared to be uncomfortable in his knowledge. "It's interesting. Did you know—"

"Jared," she interrupted him. "How did I get back here? Tell me you didn't carry me through the building."

Jared cleared his throat. "I won't lie to you."

Lisa frowned at the image that brought to mind.

"Next time, do me a favor and just give me a good shove." He started to protest, but she held up a hand. "I'm starved."

If anything, her need for nourishment should distract him she thought.

A laugh started low in his throat, erupting in a soft chuckle. He shook his dark head. "Okay, I can take a hint."

Lisa stared, fascinated. She'd never seen him laugh before. Laughter did him justice, made him appear younger, more approachable.

Rising in a natural, graceful move, he grasped one of her hands in each of his and pulled. "We have reservations at the Lighthouse for seven. That gives you thirty minutes to get ready for dinner. My private bath is through there." He waved at a door to the left of his desk.

Lisa picked up his silk jacket from where it had

slipped to the carpet. She folded it neatly and placed it over the back of a chair. Retrieving her purse from his desk, she passed him with a muttered, "Twenty minutes!"

True to her word, Lisa emerged after the specified time, makeup and hair tidily done up. As for her clothes—there was only so much you could do with wrinkles. Luckily, with today's fashions, anything went.

Jared's approval flashed from the depths of his sapphire eyes, but all he said was, "Ready?"

"Your headquarters are beautiful, Jared," she said as they made their way downstairs. "I was impressed."

"Thank you. Coming from an artist, I find that praise indeed." A half smile lifted the corner of his mouth.

"You chose the colors, didn't you?"

Surprise lifted one of his eyebrows. "What makes you say that?"

"Nothing." Lisa smiled. She didn't think he'd appreciate hearing about the clues he revealed about himself in choosing the cool surface blues and warm golden depths.

"Stop it, Lisa. There's nothing to analyze here." He looked at her through narrowed navy eyes.

She'd found his eyes acted as a key to his moods. They changed colors. From the hard slate blue of caution to the near navy of his anger, they were true barometers to his emotions. Even after knowing him for such a short time, she was learning to read the color codes. Fortunately, he didn't seem aware of the breach in his defenses, or she'd never have any indication as to what he was thinking. Like now, the deepening blue definitely told her of his displeasure.

"I did choose the color scheme, but don't look for hidden motives. I just happen to like blue and yellow."

"Exactly," she teased, shrugging as if to dismiss the subject.

Before he had an opportunity to comment, the elevator doors slid open on to the main floor and they stepped into the middle of a mild uproar. People were clustered around the reception desk, their voices pitched to override one another's, each equally intent on being heard.

Lisa blinked, unable to believe her eyes. Ashley Todd stood nose-to-nose with the security man, Farrell.

"Go ahead. Call the cops. They can search the place, but I'm not leaving here until I've found Lisa."

"Nobody's going to call the cops. I've told you, she's fine. Mr. Steele simply requested they not be interrupted. I'll inform Miss Langdon you were here. I'm sure she'll call you as soon as she gets home." Little patience remained in Farrell's tone.

"That's not good enough—"

"Ashley." Lisa broke into the confrontation.

Her friend immediately switched her attention to Lisa. It took a second for the hostility to fade from her eyes. "Lisa!" Obvious relief sounded in her voice. "Are you okay?"

"I'm fine." Lisa pulled Ashley a short distance away from the crowd. "What are you doing here?"

"I was worried about you. I've called your place every fifteen minutes for three hours. Where have you been?"

"Here. I guess Jared didn't want us disturbed because I was still sleeping."

Ashley's brown gaze flashed back and forth between Lisa and Jared. "You were sleeping?" she asked finally, incredulously. "Did he hurt you?" she demanded in a fierce whisper.

"Ashe, I'm fine." The use of the nickname, left over from their youth, was meant to relieve Ashley's mind and communicate Lisa's appreciation for her concern. "I sometimes forget the nonchalance you display to the world is only a front. That, in reality, you're fiercely protective of anything you consider yours."

"You're my family, Lisa, so if this group of thugs thinks you're a naive little thing with no one to care about you, they can think again."

The open declaration surprised Lisa. She knew how ill at ease Ashley felt about expressing her inner emotions. Her reassurances were all the more precious for that reason.

"I don't think they're in any doubt of that now," Lisa said. "Thank you, but honestly, I'm fine. Jared and I are going to dinner, we're trying to come to an understanding, get to know each other better, you know?"

"You're sure?" Ashley relaxed in the face of Lisa's apparent self-possession. "Okay, I guess I've chased after you enough for one day. But call me when you get home."

"I promise."

Lisa watched, touched, as Ashley shot a last glare in the direction of Jared, or was it Farrell? Then, drawing her purse strap over her shoulder, Ashley flipped back her long red hair and regally left the premises.

"Lisa?"

Jared stood close by her side. At no point did his body make contact with hers, yet she felt his heat along the full length of her right side and across the small of her back. She stepped forward, moving a bit away from him in an attempt to hide her shiver of awareness and create a little necessary distance.

"I'm ready."

Silence filled his Mercedes during the trip to the restaurant, each of them absorbed in their own thoughts.

Darkness shrouded the beauty of the city. Light flashed by Jared's window unobserved. Her reflections focused inward. She kept thinking of the odd facts Jared so easily quoted, secretly thrilled by all the reading he'd done on babies and pregnant women. It showed he cared.

Her thoughts were interrupted a short while later, when they reached their destination. The Lighthouse, an excellent steak and seafood restaurant, lived up to its name with a nautical theme. Fishnets draped the walls and were colorfully covered with seashells. Enchanted, Lisa especially enjoyed the old-fashioned sailing gadgetry that added to the decor.

The hostess greeted Jared then led them to a table by the window. She discreetly removed the Reserved sign, took their order for a Scotch and a Virgin Mary and left them to themselves.

From her seat, Lisa looked out at the ocean. The Lighthouse light revolved overhead. The beam swept over the waves breaking on the beach.

Entranced, she didn't hear Jared speaking until he touched her hand. Immediately, all her senses were tuned to him, shifting her attention from the beauty of the view to their hands and on to his face.

His eyes followed the opposite route—her face, their hands, the view. He broke off what he'd been saying and released her hand. Tension sizzled in the air, an awareness of each other that was getting ridiculous, particularly keeping in mind Jared's preference for noninvolvement. Something she must be aware of at all times.

The waiter approached, dispelling the tension. Orders made and their drinks before them, Lisa began to relax in Jared's company. Surprisingly, conversation flowed easily during dinner. The main topic of discussion centered on their careers. Surface talk, she thought, it gave every impression of their sharing information, but in actuality they learned nothing new about each other.

Don't push, she told herself, let him move at his own pace. Aloud she expressed her appreciation for a pleasant evening.

Jared acknowledged her thanks with a slight inclination of his head. "Is this the first time you've been to the Lighthouse?"

"No, Ashley and I came here once. We were celebrating my first commissioned sale." She smiled self-consciously. "I'm sorry about the little scene back at your office. All in all, I guess I made quite an impression there today."

"No harm done." He dismissed the incident with the wave of one lean hand. "The two of you are obviously very close."

"Yes. We were raised together in a foster home. Inevitably, they separated us, but we were lucky, we were together for several years. We may not be related by blood, but we're family just the same."

Lisa watched carefully for a change in Jared's expression. She found none. She remembered, too, how he'd found her without help from the clinic. Those facts, along with a marked lack of curiosity on his part, confirmed her suspicions.

"You had me investigated, didn't you?" His blue

eyes narrowed, an answer in itself. "I know it, and you know it, and I'm not going to pretend otherwise. I want to read the report."

He leaned slowly back in his chair, appraising her. "Why?"

"You've formed an opinion of me based on that report. I will not be my own enemy. I'm not ashamed of anything I've done, but taken out of context, some things could be misinterpreted."

"A manhunt, for instance?"

Lisa frowned, alert to the accusation behind his question. "What do you mean?"

"I mean the string of men you spent time with over the past year. How many were there? Five? Six?"

Lisa felt the color drain from her face, leaving her chilled and dazed before the color washed back in a rush of temper. She lifted her chin and met his gaze head-on.

"I don't know, I wasn't keeping count. And I don't care for your tone. So I decided to make myself more available on the social scene. I met some men, dated a few. I'll even admit I was open to meeting Mr. Right, but it wasn't a manhunt. And in case your investigator didn't specify the matter, let me make it clear, I didn't sleep with any of them!"

Her fierce denial left a tense silence hanging over the table. A waiter approached with a dessert tray. Jared waved him away.

Lisa looked down at her plate, ashamed of her tone. In this day and age, he had a perfect right to question the sexual habits of the woman carrying his child.

Still, she couldn't help being defensive. This was her child, and try as she might, she simply wasn't ready to call her baby "his." She needed time to get used to the idea, time before she'd be ready to relinquish her instinctive claim.

"I'm ready to go."

While he settled the bill, she wandered outside. The cool, damp air refreshed her after the closeness of the restaurant. Braced against the railing, she inhaled salty sea air and let the quiet rolling of the waves soothe her with its peacefulness.

Footsteps sounded on the sidewalk, then the weight of Jared's jacket descended upon her shoulders.

Grateful for the warmth, she watched the ebb and flow of the tide, trying to clear her mind of their earlier argument. It worked, to a point. With his large frame shifting restlessly beside her and his scent surrounding her, she found dismissing him impossible to do. Her awareness of him had become a constant thing.

Sometimes a person needed to face what they couldn't ignore. Reluctant to leave things as they stood between them, Lisa deliberately held out her hand.

"Let's walk."

"Lisa." The one word, her name, conveyed a wealth of meaning. It spoke of his hesitation and questioned her purpose.

She combated both with a single word of her own. "Please."

Knowing he'd probably live to regret the decision, Jared capitulated. He wrapped his fingers around hers, felt the warmth of her acceptance, the gentle squeeze of encouragement, or was it gratitude? Whichever, he determined to maintain the contact only as long as she took to climb down the uneven embankment.

Lisa broke the connection. When they reached the beach, she dropped to the sand and promptly removed her shoes and rolled up her pant legs. As she concentrated on the task, she answered one of his earlier questions.

"I was lonely. You may not be able to understand. It's hard for me to explain. I woke one morning, my twenty-ninth birthday, and it just seemed so long since I'd been a part of a real family. And the way my social life stood, I didn't see a change in the near future. So I set out to make a change."

Jared stood silently. The dark of the night hid her expression. He didn't have to ask how long she'd been alone, he knew. Only ten when the accident claimed her parents, she'd had no other family to take her in.

He watched her push to her feet and dust her sandy palms across the seat of her pants. The gesture called his attention to the sweetly rounded curves of her derriere.

"Actually, the situation was more serious than a biological clock gone haywire," she continued. "I had a uterine cyst burst. My doctor started talking hysterectomy. I told her I wanted a family. She said I better start one soon."

A quietness fell between them. Lisa strolled along the tide line, staying just out of reach of the water. Jared walked higher up on the shore, his hands tucked into his pockets. A distance of perhaps five feet separated them, but she wondered if they weren't miles apart on a different plane.

She'd opened communications between them for him, to gain his understanding. She finished the explanations for herself, to regain a sense of her own self-worth.

"Life isn't always convenient," she told him. "Mr. Right didn't show up. As time went by, I began to consider artificial insemination. I wanted a baby. A part of myself, a blood link with someone else in this world. You may think that's selfish, but I have so much love to give a child. Is it wrong to want to love?''

For a long moment the question hung in the air, dividing them. Lisa waited for Jared to say something. She felt wrung-out, not physically, but mentally, as if she had opened her heart and exposed her soul. She'd done all but reveal her most vulnerable secret, that this baby might be the only child she'd ever conceive.

The constant, muffled roar of the tide sounded loud in the thick silence separating them. A particularly rambunctious wave rushed to shore, startling Lisa into a quick retreat. She shuffled backward and reached safety only to stumble on a clump of seaweed.

She lost her balance and fell back. Worry for the baby immediately shot to mind until strong hands wrapped around her waist, catching her before she hit the ground. Through the layers of clothing and the thickness of his jacket, Jared's heat penetrated to singe her skin.

"Careful." The low, husky timbre of his voice shook her to her foundation. His breath on her cheek made her shiver as pleasure rasped along her nerve endings.

"Jared." Even as she said his name, she wondered if she did so in protest or demand.

"Lisa." Jared heaved a sigh of resignation. He owed her. The blatant honesty of her confession called for reciprocation from him. He pulled her back to rest against his sturdy length. What he had to say would come easier if he didn't have to look at her while he spilled his guts.

The comfortable feel of her in his arms had nothing to do with his decision to draw her closer. The tangy scent of salt, accented by the fresh scent of flowers, hadn't caused him to prop his chin on the top of her head. He simply meant to ensure her steadiness.

"Do you think a married couple's desire for a child is any less selfish?" he said. "More acceptable, maybe, but no less selfish."

"This wasn't an easy decision for me to make. I guess the traditionalist in me feels guilty," she said.

"I've never worried about what's considered acceptable. I want a child, and I think I'll make a good father. Growing up, I always thought I'd be a family man, husband, father, the whole bit. That changed in college. At least, the husband part did. I discovered I didn't have the temperament to cater to a woman's whims for a lifetime."

"That's rather harsh, don't you think?" she said. "College was a long time ago."

But it had been a lasting lesson, Jared thought, a painful lesson he'd learned well. "Nothing's happened to change my mind. Thanks to modern medicine, I didn't have to. I could hire someone to have my baby for me."

"That's a cynical view." The sound of the sea almost swallowed up her soft reply. "How can you believe you'll have time for a baby if you don't have time for a woman?"

"It's not a matter of having the time. I'm willing to make the adjustments necessary to raise my child. I've already started delegating most of the overseas work." The adjustment had come easier to him than he'd anticipated. A sign, he'd felt, that he'd made the right decision. "Women have their place in my life, it's just not as wife."

Lisa stiffened. "In your bed, I suppose? Sounds like a convenient justification to me."

He felt her withdrawal and told himself to release her. His body refused to comply. He liked the fit of her body pressed to his, and responded accordingly. The physical betrayal infuriated Jared. Only once since he'd been a boy in high school had he allowed his body to rule his head. He never intended to repeat the mistake.

A moment later, Lisa stood free of his touch, though less than an inch of air cushioned the distance between them. He needed to stay close, in case she required his support again.

Talk about justification, he chided himself caustically, an emotion that carried into his answer. "Decide and justify. It's one of life's eternal rhythms. We make decisions based on justifications. If we can live with the results, we go on, if we can't, we perish."

"What a frightening philosophy. Is that what you intend to pass on to your child?"

"I mean to teach my child the realities of life. Look to the future, take what you want, trust no one and protect your back."

Lisa turned, widening the cushion of space to a few inches. "I believe you get out of life what you give to it. My child will learn to look for the good in people."

"Given half a chance, people will use and discard you. You're a dreamer if you believe otherwise."

"I'd rather be a dreamer than a cynic. If you don't dream, you'll never have a dream come true. This baby is a dream-come-true for me." The sincerity of her statement rang out above the boom of the waves.

Jared fought an inner battle against an unexpected, unwanted surge of tenderness. "For me, too." He was surprised to hear his thoughts echo aloud. Embarrassed, he started to swing away, intent on retreat. He had nothing more to say.

Her hand grabbed his, stopping his exit. He felt her move closer to him as she pulled him around to face her. Moonlight lit up the beads of ocean dew misting her hair, giving the impression of a thousand diamonds being woven together by strands of gold. Her hand, soft and warm from being balled in his jacket pocket, cupped the chilled skin of his cheek, coaxing his head down to hers.

Her lips lightly brushed his forehead. "Thank you for sharing that with me." As caresses went, this one was brief, almost impersonal, yet it penetrated layers deep. Too soon, she removed her touch, depriving him of her warmth, exposing his skin to the chill in the night air.

The next thing he knew, he was brushing his lips lightly over hers. His body had taken over again, doing things he wouldn't do. The flame of desire flickered between them. Neither of them wanted it. Both of them fought it. Their resistance lasted all of thirty seconds.

Lisa's was the first to go. She deepened the kiss, letting the flame consume her inhibitions, free her passions. Lips parted, she stroked her tongue along his bottom lip, tracing the fullness, tantalizing, nibbling, playing until he swept her so close they touched everywhere.

He became the aggressor, sending the flame beyond control. It blazed, strong and bold, as she opened her mouth to his, and he explored eagerly. His tongue subdued hers to delve deep within the sweet warmth of her mouth. This was not a gentle embrace but fierce and intense with demands made and met by each of them. Hands roamed and arms tightened as their lips and mouths did the communicating.

Without warning, the mood shifted, became softer, more soothing. Lisa's arms drifted up to encircle Jared's neck and pull him closer. The first rush of passion eased. Tenderness replaced it. The slower pace allowed them to taste and learn each other.

Barriers were well and truly down, placing them on an equal footing. A man. A woman. Sharing the ancient ritual of a kiss, the preliminary embrace to the mating between the sexes.

A shudder raked Jared's solid frame. He reached around to grasp Lisa's wrists and pull them down, imprisoning them by her sides. He drew ragged breaths.

She struggled to control her own breathing. And the passion. She wanted to go on kissing him. The press of his hard muscles against her breasts, stomach and thighs kindled a need for more. But he used his superior strength to set her back on her heels, and she realized her attentions were being discouraged.

Mortified, she tucked her chin down to hide her face. Because they still stood so close, her forehead bumped into his chest. She felt the rapid beat of his heart, her first indication he wasn't totally unmoved by their embrace. The tight grip of humiliation eased marginally. Then her mind registered another portion of his anatomy reinforcing the same message.

She lifted confused eyes to scan his face. Why had he stopped? If he wanted as she did, why stop?

A loud, discordant laugh disturbed the moment.

"Hey, mister, you want to borrow my blanket?" a young voice hailed them.

"Yeah. Let's see some action," another teenager called.

There were four of them in all, Lisa saw from behind the protection of Jared's shoulder. All boys. Their average age couldn't have topped fifteen, and their comments were becoming louder, and cruder, by the minute.

"I think we should leave," she whispered.

"We will, in a minute. Stay here."

"Where are you going?"

"To have a word with our guests."

She watched him climb the beach, his tread never faltering in the sand. The boys quieted as he got closer. She didn't blame them, she'd been on the receiving end of Jared's brand of intimidation. It was something he excelled at, a language he used his whole body to speak. He reached the small group and spoke to them. A couple of the braver boys blustered a bit then they, too, stood subdued and listening.

Not a word traveled to where a curious Lisa waited, so she crept closer, wanting to hear. She was too late. Just as she attained a good vantage point, he ended the conversation. She heard only enough to know the discussion had been on manners and common courtesy rather than a threat of calling the authorities or a reminder of the curfew.

"Come on."

Jared took her elbow and led her back to the car. He was an amazing man, very complex. She began to wonder if she'd ever get to know him well enough for them to come to an understanding.

He drove her home and escorted her to the door. When the door opened, he reached inside to flip on the lights.

"It's been a long day, Jared, and an…interesting evening. Good night."

He stepped toward her, stopped, then frowned and stepped back, not allowing the opportunity for the moment to get out of hand. "Zack will bring the report by on Monday."

Without another word, he turned and disappeared into the darkness.

Chapter Five

"Lisa?" The gallery hostess's voice drifted through the speaker function of Lisa's phone. "You have a guest. Do you want to come forward, or should I send him back?"

Him? Immediately, Jared Steele's strong features flashed before her mind's eye. But why would he come here? Could he be taking their truce to heart? The thought secretly thrilled her.

So why did she feel a sudden, gut-clenching chill?

"Lisa?" the hostess prompted.

"I'll come there."

Nervously, she pushed to her feet. On the way to the show floor, she stopped to examine her reflection in a mirror by the door. Not a vain person, she nonetheless fluffed and smoothed, playing with her appearance until she quite disgusted herself. The object, after all, was not to attract Jared. They were simply getting to know each other better. Still, she defended, she wanted to be presentable.

She knew before she traveled two feet into the room that her visitor wasn't Jared Steele. This man stood taller, broader and darker than Jared. She recognized the security executive named Farrell from Steele, Inc.

As she approached him, two emotions assailed her—curiosity at his presence here and, oddly, sharp disappointment.

Farrell waited at the side of the room, away from the flow of gallery browsers, his back to the corner. A leather portfolio was tucked under one arm. Though he'd seen her, he let her come to him.

When she reached him, he nodded a greeting. "Miss Langdon."

"Mr. Farrell." Lisa offered her hand, determined to be pleasant. He had a strong grip but a gentle touch, a man who knew his own strength and controlled it accordingly. "What can I do for you?"

"You remember me. Good. Jared asked me to give you this." He extended the portfolio. The words Personal and Confidential were embossed on the front in bold, gold letters.

"Thank you." Lisa didn't ask what the folder held. She knew. Jared had said he'd send over a copy of the investigator's report.

Farrell nodded. "That's the only copy. It belongs to you now."

Lisa looked up, surprised. "Jared's giving it to me?"

"I'm giving it to you."

"You?"

"Yes."

He gave no other explanation, and Lisa wondered at

his involvement. She had the distinct impression his part went beyond errand boy.

"Did it make interesting reading?" Lisa asked, infuriated to think of her life on display for anyone to read.

Her displeasure had no effect on Farrell. "I didn't have to read the report. I compiled it."

"You must be proud."

"Jared is my friend."

"And that makes it all right?"

"No."

He gave no further justification. A stoic man, Mr. Farrell. Strangely, Lisa respected his stand. She understood the importance of friendship. "This is the only copy?"

"Yes."

"And you're giving it to me?"

"Yes."

"How does Jared feel about that?"

"I compiled the report as a favor to a friend. Jared has no say in the matter. He has access to the real thing now. If he needs to refresh his memory, he can ask you."

Was that supposed to be an apology? Though not spoken in so many words, Lisa appreciated the subtle concession. She nodded. "Thank you."

He shrugged large shoulders. "This isn't an easy situation for either Jared or you. It's the least I could do."

Lisa agreed, but graciously decided not to press the point. Their business completed, she watched Farrell move toward the door.

"Wait."

He stopped and turned. Black eyes fixed on her, he waited.

She fingered the edge of the leather portfolio, almost regretting the impulse to call him back. But since she had delayed him...

"Tell me something about Jared. Something personal, something that'll make me understand him better."

He didn't answer right away, though his hesitation was brief. "His view of women is complicated. And he's a possessive man. He won't make this easy for you. But he's fair. Play true with him, and he'll respect you for it."

Hugging the report to her, she stepped closer to him. "You haven't told me anything I don't know or haven't guessed for myself."

His massive shoulders lifted then dropped in a negligent shrug, a silent reprimand.

She should have known better than to ask the question of a friend. She shrugged too, apologetically. She'd had to try. To show there were no hard feelings, she offered her hand in farewell.

He gasped her hand, his touch oddly gentle and lingering longer than necessary as he studied her face. Finally, he released her and opened the door. Before he stepped through, he stopped and faced her. "Where he gives his affections, he's very loyal."

Lisa stared as Farrell made his exit. What was that supposed to mean? Was he indicating Jared would love his child? Or was he implying Jared might suppress his aversion to women long enough to come to terms with her?

Lisa sat back and studied her latest project. Ten-fifteen on Saturday morning, and she'd been painting since seven. The progress she'd made pleased her. This piece pleased her. She was working on what she liked to call an eveningscape, a landscape cast in the shadows of twilight.

"Just a tad more white," she muttered to herself, knowing the lighter color would deepen the effect of the shadows and brighten the effect of the rising moon. A few subtle swipes of her brush and the painting was done.

And none too soon, if her stomach had any say in the matter. She'd eaten toast and juice before she began working. The small meal usually satisfied her until noon, but not today. Her stomach had been growling for the past forty-five minutes. She wiped her hands on a rag and made her way to the kitchen.

The doorbell interrupted her search through the refrigerator. She opened the front door and stared at the sight that greeted her.

Jared stood there, all six foot two inches of him, dressed in jeans and a red polo shirt. The clothes faithfully followed the lines of his body, showing to advantage his lean strength.

But it wasn't the sight of Jared or his attire that startled Jared. It was the children that threw her. He held a boy of about two, and a girl of seven or eight had a grip on his leg tight enough to stop the flow of blood.

"Hi." Jared offered a smile.

"Hi." What now? Lisa wondered after the brilliant exchange. She stepped back and waved him into her home.

"This is my niece, Penny, and my nephew, David."

"Hello, Penny, David." Lisa smiled at each child, reaching out to trace a fingertip along the gentle slope of the baby's cheek. "My name's Lisa."

"We're going to the zoo," the little girl told her from the safety of her uncle's side.

"You are? That'll be fun." Lisa stooped to speak to Penny on her own level. "What's your favorite animal?"

"Giraffes, and elephants, and bears."

"Those are neat animals. I like bears, too, and giraffes, and elephants. Do you think you'll see any today?"

"Yes. They live at the zoo."

"They do? Even the elephants?"

Penny's grin revealed a missing front tooth. Excitement lighted familiar blue eyes. "Yes. Uncle Jared is taking us to see 'em. Do you wanna come?"

Lisa smiled and straightened, uncertain. How would Jared react to the invitation issued by his niece? She glanced at him.

He arched an eyebrow at her. "My sister's moving and needed time to pack. I thought I'd help her out by taking the kids to the zoo. Would you like to go with us?"

Lisa was overwhelmed, and quite frankly, suspicious. "Is this a test?"

"Down," David suddenly demanded, stiffening his legs and wiggling.

Jared delayed answering her while he set the boy safely on his feet and admonished him not to touch anything. When Jared faced her again, his gaze was direct. "Yes. Are you up to it?"

Lisa appreciated his honesty. She also thought this would be an excellent opportunity for each of them to see how the other responded to children.

"I'm game if you are. Give me a minute to change, and I'll be ready."

"Hello, hello. Hello!" David had found the telephone.

Jared bent to unfold strong little fingers from around the receiver.

"Please hurry," Jared said to Lisa.

The weather was beautiful for a day at the zoo, warm yet overcast so the heat wasn't too harsh. Jared suggested taking the lazy man's route by riding the bus around the park.

Lisa, with Penny's support, vetoed the idea with a grin and a firm shake of her head. "Let's walk."

"Okay, but let's start with the sections where the bus doesn't go." Jared stepped closer to Lisa and lowered his voice. "Then when kids and pregnant women get tired, we can ride the bus."

She wrinkled her nose at him, but a compromise had been reached.

"We want to save the children's zoo for last," Penny declared, hopping from foot to foot.

"Should we get a stroller for David?" Lisa asked Jared.

"He doesn't need a stroller," Penny told them. "Somebody just needs to hold his hand. Everybody hold hands. It'll be fun."

Willing to indulge, the adults both reached for a child's hand. Jared took Penny's and Lisa held David's. But Penny wasn't finished with the arrangement. "Now you guys hold hands, then it'll be boy-girl-boy-girl."

Lisa swallowed to ease her suddenly dry throat. She eyed Jared out of the corner of her eye. Too often, he'd been too close to her. She remembered every touch, and the memories made her stomach flutter.

With a complete lack of expression, he extended his hand to her, palm up. What could she do but place her hand in his and feel the warmth of his grip surround her fingers. She felt his touch all the way to her toes. By sheer force of will, she managed to ignore the tingling in her palm.

She cleared her throat and swallowed. "Shall we start with the monkeys?"

"Yeah." Penny and David shrieked their approval.

They viewed the animals on foot and then by bus, weaving through the dens, plains and jungles of San Diego's world-famous zoo.

Lisa couldn't have asked for a better buffer between Jared and herself than the children. Jared was completely comfortable with his niece and nephew. She, too, felt free to express concern and affection for the children, where she was too conscious of Jared's effect on her to be as free with him.

However, over the course of the day, she became accustomed to his touch, the occasional brush of their hips, their knees, their shoulders. There were even instances when Jared reached for her hand without Penny's prompting. No matter how casual the contact, it never lost its impact.

Lisa wanted to bypass the reptile exhibit, but with an evil grin and a yank of his hand, Jared insisted. From there it was a short walk to the children's zoo. By mutual consent, the adults stood back and watched the children play. A quiet peace came over Lisa as she witnessed the antics and joy of the excited youngsters.

There were goats and sheep of all sizes in the petting arena. Big or little, the animals reacted in one of two ways to the overeager attention of the children. The animals either stood passively and accepted the enthusiastic pats and hugs, or they bounded away as fast as their hooves could carry them.

Lisa laughed aloud and pointed for Jared's benefit to where David, showing no fear, ran up to a goat and tugged on the ear within his reach. The animal protested by jerking away. Surprised by the abrupt movement, David's big brown eyes popped wide. His startled squeal matched that of the goat's as they both scurried for safety, the goat to its mother and David to his uncle.

Jared scooped him up. "It's okay, Davie, you're okay," he soothed, a chuckle in his voice. He glanced at Lisa. "I don't know who was more spooked, David or the goat."

Not wanting to offend the boy, Lisa pressed her nose against Jared's shoulder, trying to smother her giggles. "Did you see the look on his face? His eyes were as big as saucers."

"Yeah. I better get him back into the saddle. Excuse me." Jared carried David across the yard to investigate some of the enclosures.

As Lisa watched, Penny ran up and joined her brother and uncle. They made a pretty picture, the three of them. Lisa couldn't hear what was being said. Then again, she didn't need to hear their conversation to see the concern and attention Jared lavished upon his young relatives.

Her throat tightened as she realized Jared would make a fantastic father, the type of man to be a daddy, not just a sire.

She'd seen him interact with children twice, the boys on the beach, and now his niece and nephew. On both occasions he'd shown patience, understanding and a sense of responsibility—prime characteristics for a father, and three reasons why she found him so hard to dismiss. He was also bullheaded, ruthless and determined—traits he used to maintain his defensive shield.

Because of him, her vision of the future seemed suddenly off kilter. Always before, she'd seen herself and her child making a life together. Jared's involvement changed things. Through no choice of hers or his, he was now a part of her life.

Sunlight gleamed in his near-black hair. His shirt, stretched taut shoulder to shoulder, conformed to his lean torso, and disappeared into formfitting blue jeans. Throughout the day, she'd discovered she liked how his touch made her feel. Feminine, beautiful, desirable.

She approached the trio slowly, not wanting to disturb their moment together. They were giggling over something when she reached them.

David began to dance around. "I gotta go potty."

"I have to go to the bathroom, too," Penny said.

Jared looked to Lisa to handle these demands as she had the last time the children had to go. Deciding Jared needed a more in-depth lesson in child care, she grinned and clasped Penny's hand.

"I'll take Penny. We'll meet you out front."

"Very funny." Jared swung David into his arms. "Now who's testing whom?"

Lisa gave him an arch look, confirming his allegation. "Are you up to it?"

"I'm sure I'll figure it out."

His self-assured claim followed Lisa and Penny into the ladies' room.

"Don't worry, Uncle Jared," Penny reassured her uncle, "he knows what to do."

Jared dropped the children off at his sister's house. "I'll be right back," he told her. He climbed from

the car and helped the kids as far as the front door. A
For Sale sign decorated the lawn.

His sister waited by the door. She waved and called
out her thanks, then turned and chased her small herd
into the house.

"Such energy," Lisa observed when he returned to
the car. "Where do they get it?"

"Fairies. You okay?" Jared asked. He combed gentle fingers through her tousled blond hair, returning
wayward curls to silky smoothness. Then he seemed to
realize what he was doing and pulled back his hand.

Lisa held her breath, surprised by the gesture. She
tried not to read too much into the familiar action. It
had obviously been a show of affection left over from
his day with the children.

"A little tired, but otherwise I'm fine. Fairies?" she
asked, hoping for a distraction. She met his guarded
gaze, a silent question in her eyes.

"How about some dinner?" He ignored her question.

"I'd like that."

"Good, let's go." His voice held a husky rasp. Lisa
felt it tingle through the hair on the back of her neck.

A companionable silence settled between them, broken only long enough for them to decide on a restaurant. She savored the peaceful respite. Though the
awareness, the sizzle in the air, remained a constant
thing, conversation and silences flowed with equal
comfort between them.

The restaurant Jared chose served good food and had
a cozy setting appropriate for their casual apparel. They
were sitting back relaxed after having ordered when
Lisa reintroduced the topic he'd ignored earlier.

"What were you saying about fairies?"

"Fairies? Oh. A bit of nonsense, forget it."

"No. I want to hear."

"I'm not even sure it's an official fairy tale. I think my mother made it up."

"Now you've really provoked my interest. Tell me."

"Remember, you asked for it." Absently, Jared reached for her hand. While he spoke, he played, tracing her fingers, caressing her knuckles. He watched as he did, avoiding her eyes.

"Once upon a time long ago there was a fairy. She had the special duty of awakening all the little children of the world. Morning Fairy—that was her name—was promised to Jack Frost, but instead, she fell in love with the Sandman. Morning Fairy went to Mother Nature and asked to be released from her promise. Mother Nature refused. She said promises must be kept. Morning Fairy rebelled and broke her promise anyway."

Lisa's eyes never left Jared's face as he talked. He gave his undivided attention to the linking and unlinking of their hands.

"When Mother Nature found out, she was furious. She needed to teach Morning Fairy a lesson, so she cast a powerful spell over the star-crossed lovers. The only time they would ever be able to see each other, and then only for an instant, would be when a child was between asleep and awake.

"In order to see her love as often as possible, Morning Fairy gives extra energy to the children so they tire more frequently and nap more often. She gets to see the Sandman for a brief moment each time she awakens them."

"How lovely," Lisa said, dreamy-eyed. "Romantic,

but sad. I think you're right, though, your mother made it up. You're big on fairy tales, aren't you?''

It might be her imagination, but Lisa thought his complexion darkened slightly in the imperfect lighting.

''My mother always made time to tuck the three of us into bed at night. She's not a liberated woman. Wife, hostess, mother, those are the roles she's played during her life, and she's done them all with pizzazz.''

''Three?''

''I have two sisters, one older, one younger. Joanne, David and Penny's mother, has followed in Mom's footsteps, and Mary is a junior partner in a Los Angeles law firm.'' He hesitated, his expression serious. ''I haven't told them about the baby.''

Lisa didn't know how that made her feel. What he told his family was his business. She remembered what the security man, Farrell, had said about Jared being loyal when he loved. It stood to reason, he'd want to be sure of the situation before he involved his family. She decided not to push at the moment, so she nodded and returned the topic to his sisters. ''You sound like a proud brother.''

''I am. After Dad died, I felt responsible for all of them. I was twenty-two just finishing college and on the brink of marriage.''

Marriage? Lisa blinked, surprised. She hadn't known Jared had been married. They'd discussed the fact that he wasn't married now, but what of the past? Hadn't he said his ideas of marriage had changed while he was in college?

Jared had fallen into a brooding silence. Was he thinking of his ex-wife? Or was he a widower? The conversation had held such promise, she hesitated to ask him and disturb the moment.

Too late. Whatever his thoughts, they caused his eyes to harden and his jaw to clench. No, Lisa determined, she wouldn't lose him to bitter memories.

"What happened?" she prompted softly.

His eyes refocused on her, for an instant they blazed fiercely, but she schooled her features to show calm, polite interest. He blinked. For a brief moment something flashed in his eyes, grief and then a deep sorrow.

"I ended my engagement, took over the family business, somehow managed to graduate and helped my mother and the girls when they needed me. Which wasn't all that often. They were and are strong women."

He was glossing over his role as the man of the family. She'd bet his sisters would paint an entirely different picture. So, he'd ended his engagement. Did that mean he'd never been married? And what had happened to prevent the wedding?

Was this the painful incident causing Jared to hide from his own needs?

Thrilled with the progress they'd made tonight, she recognized the time had come to change the subject. The appearance of their waiter with the dessert tray offered the perfect distraction.

"I shouldn't," she said as she looked over the delectable arrangement of luscious cakes and pies.

Jared watched Lisa exclaim over the tempting selection and cursed quietly under his breath. Rarely did he speak of his past and never of his disastrous engagement. What made tonight different?

Maybe because Lisa was so easy to talk to. She didn't play games to gain the information she wanted. She asked simple questions motivated by honest interest. He respected that about her, and found it truly frightening. In fact, the natural way they meshed scared the hell out of him.

He'd wanted to tell her about Beth, maybe then he could purge the bitter betrayal from his soul. But he refrained. His natural sense of self-preservation held strong, unbroken by the weaker, riskier urge to confide in her.

"Sir?"

Jared glanced up. The waiter nodded to the tray he held, silently asking if Jared cared for dessert. He declined, sending the waiter on his way. He saw Lisa had chosen strawberry cheesecake.

"None for you?" Lisa asked. "Good, you can help me eat mine. I couldn't resist. I love strawberries."

Unself-conscious, she scraped her chair closer to his and lifted a bite of the creamy dessert to his lips. He opened his mouth, allowing her to feed him. She smiled, awaiting his verdict. He looked into her eyes as he chewed, holding her golden gaze with his until the smile faded from her lips. Prudently, she handed him her fork and took his to use as her own.

Avoiding further eye contact, they attacked the dessert. Like teenagers, they shared the one plate, even going so far as to bicker over who should get the last bite. Lisa won, snatching the berry out from under his nose. In the true way of a winner, she gloated by closing her eyes in pure pleasure and moaning softly.

Jared nearly echoed the sound. Her sensual enjoyment of the fruit sent his blood racing. His body hardened in reaction. He'd gotten entirely too used to touching her today. She felt good, soft and warm, an addictive pleasure. He was having a hard time forgetting the feel of her in his arms.

In a gesture of forced negligence, he summoned the

waiter to request the check. The sooner he got her home the better. The better for his peace of mind, and the better for his body's comfort.

Today may not have been the brightest idea he'd ever had. He'd wanted to observe Lisa interacting with the children, though he wasn't exactly sure what he'd hoped to learn. He did know he hadn't meant to admire her so strongly. She'd handled the kids beautifully, with patience and a tolerant, guiding hand.

In the car, Lisa strapped herself in, wiggling until she got comfortable. Jared watched her from the corner of his eye. Every move she made was incredibly, unconsciously sensual.

"Thanks for inviting me today, Jared. I really enjoyed myself."

"I was glad for your help. The kids liked you."

"You sound surprised."

"I am, a little. I didn't think you had much experience with children."

"You must have skimmed the part of the report that told you about the art classes I've done for a La Mesa youth center."

"I must have. Will you be teaching again this year?"

"No. I don't want to spread myself too thin while I'm pregnant—" she wrinkled her nose "—if that's not a contradiction in terms."

Jared smiled. "I approve."

She arched an eyebrow at him. "I'm so glad."

He glanced at her then back at the road. "No need to get sarcastic. I was agreeing with you." He pulled the car to a stop. "We're here. I'll walk you to your door."

As he had before, he saw her inside and the lights on before turning to leave.

"Would you like to come in for coffee? Decaf, of course."

He shook his head, not trusting himself to stay. She was way too touchable. The indirect lighting didn't help. It shadowed her features, giving her a fragile glow. He pulled a card from his pocket and held it out to her. "Here."

"What's this?"

"An appointment card. I've made an appointment with a doctor for you this coming Friday."

She didn't say anything. She just stood there for a minute looking at the card, then she handed it back to him.

"No, thank you," she said in a tone of awful politeness.

"What's the problem?"

"No problem. I don't need an appointment or a doctor, I already have both."

"When? Who?"

She remained stubbornly silent.

"I have a right to know," he insisted.

She stared at him for another moment, her light brown eyes cool in the dim lighting. "I could argue the point, but I won't. Dr. Wilcox, a week from Tuesday."

Then she closed the door in his face.

Chapter Six

"**O**h, come on." In the gallery parking lot, Lisa struggled, unsuccessfully, to remove a stack of wrapped paintings from the trunk of her car. The top one wouldn't budge. She worked her fingers along the edges, figuring the package had to be catching on something. The painting shifted then suddenly came free, throwing her off balance.

Strong hands wrapped around her waist from behind and held her steady.

"Thank you," she breathed, shaken. She could have fallen. Her first thought went to the life growing within her. The constant sense of awareness still amazed her. She welcomed the unique responsibility, but with the wonder also came fear, especially when what she prized became threatened. This made the second time she'd almost fallen in as many weeks. She'd have to be more careful.

Turning to her rescuer, her eyes widened and she focused on a scowling Jared Steele.

"You could have been hurt. You need to be more careful."

Lisa ignored the retort that sprang to mind. No doubt he meant the less than tactful greeting as an expression of concern. "Hello to you, too."

"Are you okay?"

"Fine," she affirmed, then attempted to distract him. "I had eggs and toast for breakfast, and I have a tuna sandwich and celery sticks for lunch." Whenever he called, which had been at least once a day for the past week and a half, he wanted to know how she felt and what she'd been eating. She'd taken to answering both questions at once, saving him the trouble of asking.

"And milk?" he asked, his tone serious, but a smile played in his eyes.

"And milk," she agreed.

"Did you want these paintings out, or were you putting them in?" He took the large canvas from her, handling the bulk easily.

"Out. I'm taking them inside."

"I'll carry them for you."

"I can take one."

"No."

"Jared." Her sigh bordered on impatience. "I'm not an invalid."

"I'd like to keep it that way."

"I—" Lisa relented. The man personified stubbornness. "This way."

"I thought you did the books. Do you often handle the artwork?"

Lisa heard the underlying note of disapproval in his voice and bit her lip to control her response. Instinctively, she knew he wasn't purposely trying to rile her. It was just his protective inclinations working overtime. For her own sanity, however, she needed to set him straight.

"Jared, I'm strong and healthy and can take care of myself. I'm not going to do anything to endanger my child. A pen is the heaviest item I lift around here. Mrs. Dumond, the manager of the gallery, wants to see a sample of my work. I brought these, along with my portfolio, to show her."

"Is she thinking of displaying them?"

"Maybe. I hope these will interest her enough to warrant a position in an upcoming exhibition, but I'm not really expecting much."

"Why not?"

"Mrs. Dumond is brilliant and very particular. I've seen her change the entire mood of a painting by changing the frame."

"If she's as perceptive as you say, I'm sure she'll recognize your talent."

"How do you know I have talent? You've only seen a glimpse of my stuff." She nodded to the armload he carried.

"I've seen more than you think. Artist and book-keeper, it's a puzzling combination."

"Not really. I've always been good with numbers." She turned to him, her smile focused inward. "But art has been a part of me for as long as I can remember."

She opened the door for him then led the way to her office. She showed him around the gallery and introduced him to her co-workers, including Mrs. Dumond. When they were alone again, she confronted him. "Why are you here?"

"To drive you to the doctor's, of course."

Lisa looked at her desk clock. He was right, she'd have to leave soon or be late. Then his words sank in.

"To drive—" Speechless, Lisa stared at him, completely flabbergasted by his nerve. "You are not driving me to the doctor's."

"I am."

The man was beyond arrogant. "No."

"Yes." He glanced at his watch. "If we don't get going, we'll be late."

"I'm not going with you."

"You're being unreasonable."

"No, you're being obnoxious." Lisa grabbed her purse. He blocked her path. "Get out of my way."

"There's no sense in us both driving over there."

"That's right, there's no point in you going at all. Excuse me." She pushed past him and kept on moving until she reached her car.

"Lisa." He'd followed her. "Listen to me."

"Goodbye, Jared." The door nearly slammed on his hand. She refused to look at him as she put the car in gear and reversed out of the parking space.

Her blood simmered. The man had unbelievable gall. She'd overlooked that he'd tried to tell her what doctor to see. She'd steamed about it, but in the end she'd overlooked it. But this latest invasion of her privacy could not be brushed aside.

Her temper had not cooled by the time she reached Dr. Wilcox's office. With little patience, she filled out the forms placed before her until they called her into the back. After her examination, she dressed and joined the doctor in her office.

Dr. Wilcox was not alone. Jared sat in one of the chairs facing her desk.

"Lisa, come in," the doctor bade her, gesturing for Lisa to take a seat.

She sat, not trusting herself to say a word.

"I was just asking Mr. Steele his blood type, and I'm happy to say it's compatible with yours, so there's no problem there."

Lisa nodded. She figured she had two choices. She could make the best of this interview, or she could cause a scene she'd have to live down for the next six and a half months. The thought was enough to keep her in her seat.

"Make sure he gets all the proper forms to fill out, Doctor. There were several questions I couldn't answer regarding his background."

"Yes, we'll need a proper profile on you, Mr. Steele." Dr. Wilcox pressed a finger to a button on her phone. "Please bring me a packet of forms."

Lisa felt a perverse sense of satisfaction when the papers were placed in Jared's hands. He deserved every happy minute he'd spend filling them out.

"Lisa, you're in good health," the doctor told her. "I've a diet I'm going to give you, but it's more suggestion and example than anything else. Just use good sense. Your appetite will increase, of course, so be prepared. You can control it by eating several smaller meals throughout the day rather than overeating during the standard three meals."

Lisa reached for the proffered menu, but Jared intercepted the exchange. He examined it carefully before passing the paper on to her. Grimly, she held on to her temper.

"I'm also going to prescribe some vitamins for you," Dr. Wilcox said. "A multivitamin with added iron and calcium. I'll want to see you once a month until your eighth month, then it'll be every two weeks, and in the last month every week. Have either of you any questions?''

Lisa kept her mouth shut. Nothing was so pressing she had to know the answer while Jared sat in the next seat. She'd call later or ask questions during her next visit.

Jared had no such hesitancy. "What can she take for mild pain, headache, that kind of thing?''

For several minutes Lisa listened while they discussed the merits of non-aspirin painkillers. She made a mental note of the brands the doctor approved of. He asked another question, one Lisa had already covered with Dr. Wilcox during her examination. She glanced at her watch, trying to decide if she wanted to make an excuse and get out of here or stick around and protect her interests in the face of Jared's questions. There was no contest.

"And what about sex?''

That caught Lisa's attention. "I beg your pardon?''

"Don't be embarrassed, Lisa. It's a common question. Sex is safe. If the situation changes, I'll let you know.''

Lisa quickly pushed to her feet. "Thank you, Dr. Wilcox, you've been very helpful. I'll call your receptionist to set up my next appointment. Jared?'' She waited long enough to ensure he also intended to leave before she turned on her heel and left the office.

As she marched through the reception area and out the door, she experienced a strong sense of déjà vu as he dogged her every step.

"Lisa.'' He caught her hand. "I know you're not happy to see me, but—''

She shook her hand free. "The truce is off.''

"Don't be ridiculous. Can't you see this was important to me? This is my child, too. I have the right—"

"Don't say it." At her car, Lisa stopped and swung to face him. "I also have rights. One of which is the right to privacy. When you can learn to respect that, we'll talk again."

She dug for her keys, her movements agitated and futile. Anger gripped her until she trembled with the emotion. Her fingers shook so badly when she finally located the keys, she couldn't fit the door key into the lock.

"Let me help you." Jared extended his hand, braving her mood to assist her.

She snatched the keys from his reach. "I can do it. I can walk and carry things. I know how to eat sensibly. I can ask my own questions. And my love life is none of your business. Now, get out of my face before I get violent."

Their eyes clashed in fierce challenge, hers defiant, his unreadable. Whatever his hidden thoughts, he chose not to push her. A wise decision on his part.

He stepped back a pace, shoved his hands in his pants pockets and said, "I'll call you."

"No." With more determination than grace, she managed to open her door and climb into the car. "Let *me* call *you*."

"I still can't believe you threatened him with violence. I mean, you of all people." Ashley shook her head as she laughed. She sat a short distance away, on the floor of Lisa's living room. They were eating popcorn and watching a rental movie.

"I felt violent at the time," Lisa said. "The man

asked my doctor if I could have sex. Why? Neither of us would consider complicating this situation in that way. And I can't see him letting another man come within ten feet of me."

"Obviously, you didn't ask him. How long ago did this altercation occur? I'm definitely going to have to close the New York sale. I'm missing all the good stuff."

"About a week and a half ago, and I haven't heard from him since, except for those flowers. They came this morning."

Ashley glanced at the exotic arrangement in the center of Lisa's small dining-room table. "Lovely."

"It's a peace lily."

"I'm impressed. Are you going to call him?"

Lisa shrugged. "I'm thinking about it."

A knowing look came her way. "Testing him, are you?"

Lisa shrugged. "Maybe. A little. But he deserves it. You should see the report he had done on me."

"What kind of report?"

"Every kind of report imaginable. Here, let me show you." Lisa retrieved the leather portfolio from her bedroom, handing it to Ashley when she returned to the living room. "A credit report, a DMV printout, a police report, bank statements, my employment history. There's even a document from the FBI stating I have no file."

Ashley flipped through the pages. "This is incredible. Here's a report from the county on you, every foster home you've ever lived in is listed. I didn't think this information was available to the public."

"It's not. Zack Farrell is nothing if not thorough. He must have connections in very high places."

"Farrell?" Ashley wrinkled her nose. "I should have known. The man has the manners of a gestapo guard. He probably used intimidation to get the information he wanted."

Lisa grinned at her friend's reaction. "I'd forgotten you two have met. I can see he made a lasting impression on you."

Ashley ignored the leading comment. She continued to thumb through the contents of the file. "This is against the law, you know. You could take them to court."

"I don't want to do that. Our situation is precarious enough without allowing petty grievances to complicate things."

"You're too easy on the bums. I'd sue the pants off them. You can't let Jared get away with this. He owes you."

"I tried to get Zack to reciprocate with some information about Jared, but it was no go."

"Why am I not surprised?"

"Because you don't like Zack, but I think I do. I respect a man who keeps his friend's secrets. What am I going to do, Ashe? How can I make sure he gets the point? I can't have him invading my privacy like he has been."

Ashley picked through the kernels in the bottom of the bowl. "Invade his back."

"How? I wouldn't feel right hiring my own private investigator."

"You don't have to actually hire anybody, just threaten to. Or, better yet, ask Jared for the information."

Lisa clapped her hands in approval. "I like it. I'll demand to see everything, financial reports, school transcripts, a family history and a full health report from his doctor.''

"Now you're talking. When?''

"Saturday, that gives me a couple of days to prepare. I've never been to his condo. I might as well make it a full-scale invasion.''

"I like your style.'' Ashley pinned her with an arch look. "Have you given any more thought to speaking with a lawyer?''

Lisa chewed her bottom lip. "I've thought about it.''

"And?''

"And I don't know. Sure, Jared is arrogant, stubborn and overly protective, but I don't believe he'd intentionally hurt me. And he's wealthy, Ashe. If this case went to court, I could lose.''

"Oh, Lisa.'' Ashley scooted close to put her arm around Lisa. "I know you're scared, but you have to protect yourself. Do you think Jared hasn't spoken to his lawyers?'' Ashley shook her head. "You can bet he knows his legal position, which could be why he hasn't pursued a legal approach. After all, you are the mother, and with your medical history, this could be the only baby you ever have. A jury would have to be inhumane to take your child away from you.''

"Okay.'' Lisa hoped Ashley was right. "Set up an appointment for me with your lawyer, but I just want to talk. And you have to come with me.''

Ashley's arm tightened around Lisa. Reassurance and love flowed through the contact. "You're doing the right thing, Lisa. Trust me, you won't regret this decision.''

Lisa regretted her decision, and that was the least of the emotions she felt as, on Friday afternoon, she sat in leather comfort in an expensive wood-paneled office. The scents of fresh-brewed coffee and old cigars permeated the air, causing her stomach to churn.

Ashley, decked out in a red leather blazer and a black miniskirt, occupied a matching chair to Lisa's left.

They'd been in the lawyer's office for twenty shell-shocked minutes. Edward Hatchard wasn't Ashley's friend but a senior partner in her friend's firm. He'd insisted he be the one to speak to Lisa.

At first she'd objected to the personal nature of his questions, but he'd overruled her, saying he needed to know all the facts. He also pointed out the opposition would be less kind in their questioning of her.

He made her feel sordid, cheap and easy. She didn't think anyone could make her feel worse.

Lisa stared at the big man with thinning red hair and a crooked nose, stunned into silence.

Ashley had no such problem. She shot to her feet in fiery protest. "That's enough. Miss Langdon came here today for advice, not to be interrogated. I fail to see what her preferred method of birth control has to do with her rights in a custody battle."

"Please be seated, Miss Todd. If this case reaches a courtroom, Miss Langdon's social and sexual mores will come under close scrutiny. We must be prepared."

"Mr. Hatchard—" Lisa made a grab at claiming control of the interview "—I really have no desire to see the inside of a courtroom. I came here to determine my legal position."

"Well, as to that, Miss Langdon, I can't possibly say. Many surrogate cases have favored the birth mother, but an equal number have decided for the donor couple. In this case, you're two-thirds of that equation, which should act in your favor. However, Mr. Steele is an influential man who did not grant you indiscriminate use of his sperm.''

"Enough of the double talk, Hatchard," Ashley cut in. "We already know the situation, what we want to know is the outcome."

"There are no guarantees, of course, but I believe Miss Langdon has a solid case against the clinic. We can expect a lucrative settlement from them. The custody issue has less potential. I'd advocate for joint custody. That way, we can hit Steele up for child support and punitive damages. Of course, with the public behind you—"

Lisa had heard enough. She rose on shaky legs and, with forced politeness, extended her hand to the lawyer. "Thank you for your time. I have to leave now."

Ashley, having skipped the pleasantries, led the way out the door and to the elevator. When the doors closed behind them, she enveloped Lisa in a hug. "I'm so sorry."

"It's not your fault." Lisa returned the comforting embrace before stepping back a pace. "You were right, this was something I had to do. But I don't want a settlement. Jared is no more responsible for the situation we find ourselves in than I am. Just because he has money doesn't mean he should be made to pay. And I don't want my private life turned into a circus."

"What are you going to do?" Ashley asked.

"I'm going to go see Jared tomorrow as I planned. If joint custody is the probable outcome of a court case, we should be able to work that out by ourselves."

Soft bells trilled, announcing Lisa's third-floor destination. The elevator doors fell silently open, and she stepped into a plush corridor. She glanced at her watch, nine-fifteen, Saturday morning. Not too early, she thought, to confront Jared. Even for the weekend, she had him pegged as an early riser.

Looking up and down the hall, she saw she had the choice of two doors, one to the north, the other to the south. She glanced at the white business card Jared had given her with his personal information scribbled on it. Under his home phone number, he'd written his address, but there was no distinction besides third floor.

She'd used the card to bypass security. Waiting for a couple of tenants to come along, she asked for directions then walked with the two women past security into the elevator, shamelessly sneaking into the building.

Now she chose the door to the south. Before knocking, she took several deep, heartening breaths. Then, with her resolve strengthened, she rapped on the solid oak door. While she waited, she considered the growth of their relationship over the past two months. Or was she being optimistic to use the word *growth?*

She liked to think of herself as a tolerant person, or failing that, a flexible person. Both characteristics had been pushed to the limit. She felt good about her decision to take things into her own hands, to give Jared a taste of his own medicine.

After a minute, she knocked again. Immediately, the door swung in to reveal a plump, dark-haired woman with a sweater over her arm and a purse in her hand. "Yes?"

"I'm here to see Jared Steele," Lisa stated, wondering if she had the wrong suite.

"He's in. I was just leaving, but I'll tell him you're here. Who may I say is calling?"

Before Lisa had the opportunity to answer, Jared emerged from a room down the hall. He wore a silk robe, damp in places from a recent shower. His hair clung in wet curls against his neck. When he spied her in the doorway, a frown creased his forehead.

"Hello." Lisa turned on her brightest smile and stepped past the woman into the hallway.

Jared closed the distance between them, his eyes concerned. "What's wrong, Lisa?"

"Nothing. I received your flowers, and I decided we needed to talk."

The lines across his forehead deepened. "Everything's all right with the baby?"

Lisa's smile faltered. She hadn't expected him to show such concern. "The baby's just fine."

"And you're okay?"

"Yes."

The expression in his eyes changed, chilled. "You should have called."

"Yes, well, I didn't. And before you ask, I snuck past security." She remembered her purpose for being there and threw a few extra watts into her smile. "If we're going to reinstate our truce, there are some things I'll need to have from you. I've compiled a list." She handed him the paper with her demands then spun into the living room behind her. "I'll wait in here while you dress."

"What the—?" Jared took one look at the list then reached out to stop her. Long, strong fingers wrapped around her wrist, not tight enough to hurt but secure enough to ensure she followed where he led. "No, you won't wait here. Come with me."

Back in the hall there was no sign of the woman,

obviously his housekeeper. She'd quickly made herself scarce.

Jared headed into the depths of the condo. The door he'd come through earlier stood open, offering no obstacle as he stormed into his bedroom. The room, done in beige and brown, hardwood and brass, was as boldly masculine as its occupant.

"What the hell do you think you're doing? Coming here? Making demands?" While he raged, Jared tore off his robe with a savage movement, then stalked in skintight knit boxers to the wall-length wardrobe.

The gray knit hugged his body in ways that made Lisa's mouth water. She sank into a nearby chair to watch unashamedly, forgetting for a moment her reasons for being there.

"I don't hear from you for almost two weeks and then you throw something like this at me." He tossed a pair of jeans across the bed. A pale blue shirt followed close behind. Anger accented every motion.

"You have no right barging in here," he went on. "Getting acquainted doesn't mean invading each other's privacy."

Lisa only half heard him. She was too busy enjoying the private performance. Bronze muscles bunched and relaxed at the simple task of dressing. Even angry, he moved with grace and an economy of movement that was beautiful to watch.

As an artist, she recognized the perfection of his proportions, automatically assessed dimensions and measurements. But as Lisa, the woman, she knew desire. He was broad where a man should be broad, slim where a man should be slim, and bulged, oh yeah, where a man should bulge. She doubted she'd ever be able to manage the objectivity necessary to sketch him.

His deep, angry tones washed over her as she watched his fluid movements. Beads of moisture glistened in the dark hair covering his chest, and Lisa fought the unexpected longing to lick the wetness from his skin. Where the erotic impulse came from, she couldn't say, but the desire didn't shock her.

He pulled on his jeans, then stretched across the bed to retrieve his shirt from the far side. Her attention shifted with the donning of his pants from the long, hair-roughened length of his legs to the broad, muscular width of his shoulders.

But as more and more of his body disappeared from her view, more and more of what he said began to penetrate her sensual preoccupation.

Words such as *nosy* and *snooping* infiltrated at first. And she seemed to recall hearing something about invasions of privacy in his earlier rumblings. When he started in on rights and responsibilities, he gained her full attention.

"…presume upon the situation by coming here unannounced. You're pregnant with my child, that's a fact. It doesn't give you an open invitation to my home. I was afraid something like this would happen."

Dressed except for his shirt hanging open, he stood, hands on hips, and glared at her in cool disgust.

Lisa rose slowly from the chair. She had had enough. She met his contemptuous glare full on and spoke through clenched teeth.

"You've come and gone in my life as you please with no warning and no explanations. Not only have you trespassed into my background, you've come to my home and tried to claim my baby as well. You consistently call me up and interrogate me about what I'm doing, where I've been and what I'm eating. If that's not an invasion of privacy, I don't know what is. I've accepted it, and you, because I respected my child's right to know his father.

"I didn't call before coming here today, and I made up that list because you needed to be taught a lesson. I'm not one of your possessions. You can't continue to invade my life as you have without some form of reciprocation."

Throughout her explanation, Jared's stance remained the same—unrelenting. Exasperation added to Lisa's anger, but she fought to control it. She tried taking deep, calming breaths. "Look, I know you're hurting from something in your past—"

"How?" he attacked. "Who's been talking about my past?"

"Nobody talked to me. Every word out of your mouth, every controlled move you make, your whole attitude is a protective shield against further hurt."

"You don't know what you're talking about."

"I do. Pain is pain, whatever the cause."

He ran an exasperated hand through his hair. "I knew this would happen. I knew you'd want more than I'm willing to give."

"You know nothing about me or what I want. I'm making no claim on you. I didn't ask for you to come knocking on my door. I planned on having my baby alone." A gesture of her hand indicted his tall, virile person. "You were a complete surprise. Unexpected—yet not totally unwelcome. Having a baby for the first time, it's kind of scary, you know?"

She received no response, not even the inclination of his head. Discouraged, she wondered why she bothered, why she continued to fight.

For her baby, she reminded herself. Because this man was her child's father.

"I thought I'd at least have someone with whom to share the experience. But right away you took that from me. There would be no relationship between us, which was ridiculous. How can we have a child together without having some kind of relationship?"

Closing her eyes against the unfeeling look in his gaze, she reviewed the past weeks in her mind. When she looked at him again, she feared the despair she couldn't deny would be revealed to him.

"Let me tell you, Jared Steele, knowing the contents of my credit report, or even the state of my health, doesn't get the job done."

"I've spoken to you almost every day."

She waved his comment away. "That doesn't count. All you learned about me during those calls is what I ate." He just wasn't getting it. "Look, I know you didn't plan on me, either. But the reality is, I'm not going to go away. Not for money, and not to make it easy for you."

"Nothing about this situation has been easy since you became involved." The corner of his mouth lifted in a sneer that had Lisa gritting her teeth.

"Since I conceived, you mean. Without me there is no baby!"

His expression grew grimmer, something she wouldn't have thought possible. This conversation wasn't going as she'd hoped, and she didn't know how to regain control. If she'd ever had control.

It was time for some straight talk.

"You're going to have to make a decision," she told him. "Either you forget about the baby and let me fade quietly out of your life, or you make a commitment.

Start a real relationship that will allow us to raise our child as a team, together, as partners. It's your choice.''

Lisa held her breath, waiting for his reaction. He didn't look pleased. Too bad! The end of her tether was within touching distance. And her doctor had warned her against added stress. Enough changes were occurring within her body, she didn't need the emotional strain of an uncertain alliance with this man.

Muscles tense, eyes alert, Jared contemplated her ultimatum. ''What if I don't agree with those choices?'' He finally demanded. ''What if I decide to take you to court to claim sole guardianship of my child?''

''No!'' The cry came from the very core of her soul. ''You can't do that.''

She struggled to get herself under control. The meeting with the lawyer fresh in her mind, she knew the importance of keeping her wits about her. ''I know my rights,'' she insisted. ''This child is mine.''

His blue eyes narrowed to mere slits. ''And mine.''

''This wouldn't be one of your everyday cases, Jared,'' Lisa pointed out desperately. ''It could drag on for weeks, even months. A very private area of our lives would be exposed to the vicious scrutiny of the media. The decision to have my baby by artificial means was a difficult one for me to make. In the end, it was right for me, but it isn't something I want broadcast on a tabloid TV show.''

Hoping she read his defensive expression correctly, she offered one last argument. ''You won't take the issue to court. Embarrassment aside, you would never subject your child or your family to the pain of such a trial.''

Stalemate.

They faced off, one against the other. Their child too important to each of them for either to relent.

His challenging silence infuriated Lisa. The power of her emotions, raw and exposed, kept her quiet while the more rational side of her nature fought to gain calm. The effort proved futile. From the moment she walked through the door, she'd been jerked from one emotional extreme to the other. Now, in the battle of calm over fury, fury won.

"You're bluffing, Jared. Threatening me in another of your tests, and it makes me furious. How dare you propose taking my baby from me when the child means nothing more to you than a signature on a contract?"

Something—pain?—flickered in his eyes then disappeared, his expression as cold and harsh as the ugly epithet he called her.

Lisa reeled from the insult.

"No," she denied, losing the fragile hold she held on her control. "Just a mother protecting her child."

"From the father?" he demanded.

"If necessary."

"No."

"Yes." The bitter taste of gall filled her mouth and tears burned the back of her eyes. "And your talk of court cases and single custody makes it necessary. You, with your millions behind you. It's easy to make accusations and threats when you have the funds to buy what you want." The words fell fast and raging hot. Too fast to be planned. Too hot to be given much thought.

She needed to see an emotional response from him, even if she had to shock it out of him. She'd reached the point where looking into his stern, unrevealing features, she lost all sense of reason. "This is a new millennium. A woman's body belongs to herself. I should just end it—''

Lisa clamped a hand over her mouth. Eyes wide, she began to tremble. She longed to call back the words, but they echoed and reechoed through her mind.

The tears she'd held back moments before fell unheeded down her face. Fear knifed through her, leaving shock in its wake. Slowly, her hands cradled over her belly, she sank to the floor.

The need to protect her unborn child sapped Lisa's strength, overrode all other emotions. She rocked listlessly, holding herself tightly, silently, striving for forgiveness from herself, from Jared. Unable to look him in the eye, she buried her face in her hands.

Chapter Seven

Concern for Lisa swept away Jared's anger. In the face of her distress, he didn't hesitate. He knew he risked rejection, but he couldn't stand by while she suffered.

He stepped forward and swung her into his arms. Sitting in the chair she'd vacated, he arranged her on his lap and began a gentle rocking motion. She seemed to welcome the sheltering hold as her shivering body burrowed into the warmth of his.

"I'm sorry," she whispered, her breath catching on a sob. "S-so sorry."

He was sorry, too. He'd been a jerk, more than a jerk, and he knew it.

"It's okay," he reassured her, his voice unnaturally husky even to his own ears. "The baby is safe, you're keeping the baby safe for us inside you. Nothing can happen to our child."

"I didn't mean what I said. I'd never hurt the baby, honest I wouldn't."

"Of course not," he said, thinking of the past and the woman who aborted a child with premeditated malice. What a contrast between Beth and Lisa, who shook in despair at the mere mention of abortion.

He tightened his arms as she continued to cry, smoothing a hand over the silky strands of her blond hair in a soothing caress. The petal-soft scent of wildflowers floated up to him, bringing to mind the delicate blossoms that fought a constant battle against the elements and won.

Lisa possessed the same fragile strength, but now she fought a silent battle of her own. He knew she feared the repercussions of her careless words. He felt her pain as his own. Because he'd driven her to this point—first by overreacting then by denying her plea for understanding, and finally by threatening her.

The need to comfort overcame lesser emotions, such as guilt and shame. The last of his misplaced anger evaporated with the feel of her soft body cuddled next to his. She needed the reassurance only he could give her.

"Please don't cry." He mouthed the plea against the curve of her neck. "It breaks me up inside when you cry."

Muffled sobs filled the room, shuddering through Lisa's limbs as she tried to stem her tears. An unfamiliar sensation of security surrounded her in Jared's comforting embrace, easing the ball of distress in the pit of her stomach.

"Everything's going to be okay," he whispered.

Then he started to whisper nonsense, simple and sweet. He nibbled tenderly on her ear. Slowly, the tension eased out of her body and the dampness dried on her cheeks.

''Fool.'' Self-conscious, she sat up.

''Better?'' He lifted a finger to trace the path of a lingering teardrop.

Lisa thought about his question. Logically, she knew her reaction bordered on the ridiculous, but emotionally the words weren't so easy to dismiss. Finally, she nodded.

Impulsively, she pressed forward in his lap and nuzzled a kiss to the sensitive skin below his right ear. ''Thank you.''

A masculine knuckle shifted the angle of her head, and his mouth slanted across hers. Gratitude played no part in the kiss. The force was desire, pure and simple, as was her response. What they'd tried to ignore from the beginning would no longer be denied. The awareness between them ignited, exploding with all the steamy pressure of a geyser.

He invaded her mouth with the hot mist of his breath and the seductive thrust of his tongue. Lisa met and returned the demanding strokes, matching his need with her own. Her hands found the open edges of his shirt and pushed the intrusive garment from his shoulders. His hot, hard, satin-smooth muscles flexed under her touch.

Her senses buzzed. Her nerves sizzled. She drifted, lost in the heat of a sensual high. Natural. Fierce. Passionate.

Arms curved around Jared's waist, her fingers testing the texture of his flesh, Lisa did what she'd wanted to do earlier. She licked up a bead of moisture nestled in the dark chest hair.

"Mmm..." An appreciative groan escaped her de-sire-clenched throat.

"Lisa." With an answering growl, Jared again claimed her mouth. She tasted so good, warm and sweet and eager. The scent of her flower perfume weaved around him, enticing him to search out her pulse points. Her blood raced to the same beat as his. Under his mouth, his fingers, he felt the pounding pace and sought to rationalize the moment.

This woman's touch pushed him to the point of no return faster than any other woman he'd known. He mustn't pass that point without her consent. Though he needed her.

Immediately, Jared denied the thought. He grasped her shoulders and held her away, creating distance be-tween them even as he acknowledged a driving urge to mentally, as well as physically, make his baby real. He fought to reject his need. He didn't want this, no matter how good, how right having her in his arms felt.

Lisa looked at him, her beautiful eyes confused at the interruption. Slowly, through the passion-fogged depths, her gaze focused on him.

"Please, Jared. Make love to me."

"Lisa." He shook his head, stalling. Fighting her, fighting himself. "Do you know what you're asking?"

"I know exactly what I'm asking." Her tone, firm if slightly husky, held certainty. Her emotions were un-der control. "I could never regret this, Jared. Make a baby with me?"

He felt the plea to the center of his heart. His throat tightened, his pulse sped and his loins ached. When she moved into his arms, there was no going back. He lifted her and carried her to his bed.

His eyes never leaving hers, he stepped back to remove the rest of his clothes. Lisa watched as she had before, but this time anticipation overpowered appreciation. He came to her magnificently nude, magnificently aroused. Her body reached for him, closed around him, held him. She lifted her head and met his descending mouth. Their lips fused, bonded by mutual hunger.

Then, to her delight, his mouth began to wander. The corner of her mouth received a kiss, the line of her jaw a nibble, and the sensitive length of her neck suffered the fiery torture of his tongue tracing a path down to where her blouse prevented him from going farther.

Rising to rest on his elbow, Jared dealt with the obstacle in simple unhurried movements. One button at a time, he slowly parted the sides of her blouse. Under the silk, he found an enticing display of peach lace and creamy skin.

"You're so lovely."

Lowering his head, he kissed first one peach-covered crest and then the other, drawing a gasp from Lisa.

He lifted his head. "Tender?"

"Yes, but wonderful." Her swollen, sensitized breasts bloomed under his soft touch.

He continued undressing her, item by item until she was as naked as he. Each newly uncovered section of skin received urgent, dedicated attention. He left her breathless, needful.

The silly verses he'd used to distract and comfort were nothing compared to the erotic promises he breathed against her skin. Promises he fulfilled with gentleness when care was needed and hard driving passion when nothing else would do.

He joined their bodies with a slow, penetrating tenderness that echoed through all his movements. Never would Lisa forget the look of gratification his eyes held when his first stroke buried him deep within her. She, too, felt complete, whole, as if the other half of herself had been found.

He moved, and she moaned in pleasure. He thrust, and she surged to meet him. He withdrew, and she felt an emptiness she'd never experienced before and never wanted to feel again. The tension grew, building until it exploded in wave after wave of exquisite satisfaction.

Time passed, seconds, minutes, an hour. They lay without moving. Lisa curled into Jared, her head resting on his chest. She was afraid to disturb the moment, afraid he already regretted the shared intimacy. With every breath he took, she felt his withdrawal become more complete.

He wanted no part of the closeness she'd found so satisfying. He'd made that clear from the very beginning.

Stop it, she admonished, trying to convince herself she had no way of knowing what he was thinking. After all, he hadn't tried to throw her out or anything. In fact, he hadn't so much as moved since they'd settled into their present positions. He'd slept for a while, yet she knew he'd been awake for some time. With her head rising and falling to the pattern of his breathing, she'd been able to gauge when his breaths changed from sleep to wakefulness.

She caught herself up, why worry about his reaction when she'd be better occupied examining her own? Did she regret giving herself to Jared?

Not for a minute. Besides their lovemaking being the most shatteringly beautiful event of her life, how could she regret the act that should have been the conception of her child?

Two months ago, in a clinical environment with a mechanical procedure, an anonymous man's seed found a fertile egg within her womb. Biologically, a new life began. Today, two people came together in comfort and need. They'd touched and explored and given to each other the essence of life. Emotionally, a baby was created.

As a result, she needed more from Jared than a return to their customary armed truce. She craved harmony between them, and time unrelated to the situation forcing them together.

Jared stirred beneath her. She lifted her head and looked down at him. Immediately, shutters fell to shield the expression in his eyes. He was retreating from her. Lisa made a bid to stop it. "Give me today."

He lowered straight eyebrows in a frown of resistance. His blue eyes became leery. "I don't—"

"Please? Give us this time together. Just you and me. No work, no arguing, no talk of the baby. And no questions. Just you, me and the sunshine."

Her plea tempted Jared despite the warning bells clanging in the back of his mind. He'd held her close for the past hour because he liked the feel of her in his arms. And because he wanted to delay a return to reality. One moment every nerve urged him to push her away, and in the next he longed to grasp her so tightly she'd never get away.

Instead, he lay without moving as his mind warred with his—what? He refused to acknowledge it as his heart.

Could he afford to take today?

For better or worse, he found he couldn't deny her. "Okay, we'll take today."

Joy brought a sparkle to her hazel eyes. "Thank you." She dropped a quick kiss on his cheek.

"Ah-ah." He shook a finger at her. "None of that now. That's what set us off last time."

"Are you making no touching one of the rules of the day?"

He gave her an arch look. "Do I look like a masochist to you?"

The words brought to mind memories of another time and another place. Not since the betrayal in college had he felt so vulnerable. Not again, he promised himself, never again.

When he resumed speaking, his voice lost all traces of teasing. "Sure we can pretend to be lovers." He ignored her frown. And the anxiety in her eyes. "But if you want to do something besides screw, I suggest you give serious thought to vacating this bed."

His crude warning and cold tone slapped Lisa in the face. The pain hit hard and deep. She turned and swung her legs off the bed, her gaze searching for her clothes. Pride forced her to make light of her retreat.

"Hey, it was a bad idea," she said. "A complete waste of time. Forget I ever mentioned anything."

She grabbed up a handful of clothes, and using them to shield her body, she headed for the nearest door.

It opened into a closet.

"Where's the bathroom?" Her composure gone, her voice broke on the last word.

Ashamed of his behavior, Jared cursed. He'd seen the hurt reflected on her face and done nothing to stop her flight from the bed. But even he couldn't withstand her painful embarrassment at the bumbled escape attempt.

He should have anticipated the sensitivity of her

feelings, made all the more so because of her pregnancy. Because he hadn't, or more accurately, because he'd deliberately provoked her when he shouldn't have, he went to her and enfolded her in his arms. The naked length of her back pressed to the naked length of his front.

"I'm a jerk."

"Let me go." Twisting and turning, she fought against the intimate embrace. His arms tightened, pulling her closer. She stopped the futile wiggling as two things became obvious—she wasn't going anywhere until he let her go, and her efforts were having a provocative effect on him.

Standing still, she counted to ten. Finally, her normal spirited nature reasserted itself. She swung around to face him.

"You are a jerk." She agreed. "What's the matter with you, anyway? We just made love. Is it so wrong for me to want to spend some time with you?"

"No. Of course not. I'm sorry." He punctuated his sentences by feathering brief kisses over the stubborn jut of her chin. "I *want* to spend the day with you."

She shook her head. "It wouldn't work."

"No work, remember?"

He rocked her gently in his arms, a soft side-to-side sway. The motion soothed as it was intended to. The corners of her mouth lifted in a reluctant smile. He could be charming.

She relaxed against him, his solid strength supporting her easily. He smelled of sweat and spice, the familiar aromas of his aftershave and their recent activities. She realized she must have a similar earthy scent.

"Okay. But, I need to shower first."

"No." He corrected, "*We* need to shower."

"Hmm, I think I like the sound of that."

"Oh, you'll like it. I can guarantee it." He released her except for the clasp of their hands, then drew her across the room to the bathroom....

With a kiss and the promise of breakfast, Jared left the bedroom suite for the kitchen.

Lisa smiled as she watched him leave the room. He'd been very gentle with her since he'd apologized. His passion and generosity in the shower gave her hope that the day might be a success.

Dressed again in her shirt and pants, she looked around for a brush to use on her hair. A framed picture on a table in front of the window caught her eye.

Curious, she moved closer and picked up the black lacquer frame. The five-by-seven photograph showed the silhouette of a boy and his father walking hand in hand into the sunset. The words *Was it worth it?* were scrawled across the bottom left-hand corner in angry black slashes.

Lisa wondered at the significance of the picture and the inscription. The writing did not belong to Jared. She'd seen his writing several times and didn't recognize this as his. But the sentiment portrayed in the picture certainly reflected Jared's plans for the future, even as the inscription questioned the validity of his plans.

Of course, considering everything that had happened since he'd put into action his plans to have a child, the question held merit. Too bad the rules of the day prevented her from asking Jared about the picture.

With mixed feelings she returned the photograph to its place on the table. She felt both touched and threatened by the evidence of Jared's dedicated pursuit of parenthood.

If only his plans had included the full family circle. But then she probably would never have met him. The thought brought a strange sadness to her heart. One she wasn't prepared to explore at the moment. Instead, she found a brush in a drawer in the bathroom and completed her toilet before joining Jared in the kitchen.

To her astonishment the room held no surprises for him. He diced and sliced, washed and beat, spiced and sautéed to produce a mouthwateringly perfect menu of golden-brown omelette, orange slices sprinkled with sugar and cinnamon, hash-brown potatoes and freshly perked decaffeinated coffee.

They carried their feast onto the balcony, leaving behind a lavish mess. Lisa took heart in the fact that efficient, controlled Jared was a messy cook.

She froze in the open doorway, her plate in hand, looking from the kitchen to the man on the patio. She loved him.

It scared her to admit it, but she couldn't deny her feelings any longer and remain honest with herself.

When had he gotten to her? Maybe when they'd been on the beach in the moonlight. Or possibly when she'd called her doctor to schedule her next appointment and learned that after she'd stormed off, Jared had returned to the office and completed the numerous forms given to him. Or it could have been the sight of Jared scooping a frightened David into his arms.

In truth, her love was the result of all those incidents and more.

More than ever, she wished the rules of the day didn't exist. She wanted to talk to him, to tell him of her feelings. Only the certain knowledge it would be a mistake stopped her. She dared not reveal her love. Not anytime in the near future. He didn't want to know and probably wouldn't believe her if she did confess her feelings.

She ached as never before to know the mystery of his past. What had caused him to cut himself off so completely on an emotional scale?

She might never know.

So she lacked the facts and the courage to voice her emotions. Actions were still hers to use. Everyone knew actions spoke louder than words anyway.

A person had five senses, and being denied the more obvious verbal approach, she'd use the other four to express her feelings. From now on, whenever she spent time with Jared, he'd see, taste, smell and feel the strength of her love. Subtly, of course. She didn't want to bombard the man—or he'd steel up behind his brick wall and never come out.

He sat at the terrace table, the sea breeze lifting his dark hair, a black polo shirt stretched taut across his shoulders. His sheer male presence drew her. She wanted to take his hand and lead him back to the bedroom.

He looked up at her and smiled, waving her into the seat across from him.

"Come on out, the weather's fine."

The salty ocean air sharpened her appetite. A cool breeze offset the baking rays of the sun, and from a distance she heard the muted roar of the surf.

Lisa stole every opportunity she could to touch Jared, from the meeting of fingers when she passed the salt, to the angling of her legs so that her knee rested against his, to the casual flicking away of imaginary crumbs from his muscular forearm.

At first he shied away, unconsciously she was sure. She just backed off until he relaxed then she made contact again in a retreat-and-advance campaign that accustomed him to her touch. The easy compatibility boded well for the rest of the day.

"Where do you want to go?" Jared asked a short time later as he pulled out of the garage.

Lisa shrugged. "Wherever you want." She didn't care what they did as long as they did it together. That left them free to go where the mood struck them.

During the heat of the day, Lisa pulled Jared into the cool darkness of a movie theater, where she learned he too liked action movies. Harrison Ford had never been better, and she only had to bury her face against Jared's shoulder twice during the film.

After sitting for two hours, Jared felt like some exercise so she agreed to learn how to play golf. He instructed and Lisa tried, but somewhere between his words and her application the execution suffered. In the end, she traded her caddie services for dinner at her favorite Mexican café in Old Town. He teased her about her tourist tendencies until he tasted the excellent food.

It wasn't an easy day for Jared. He tried, as did Lisa, to stick to the rules, but try as he might, he couldn't forget the existence of his child, even for so short a time.

There were reminders everywhere. After dinner, as they strolled through Old Town, a man stopped Jared to ask for directions. Lisa wandered ahead. When he caught up to her, she stood in front of an antique shop, an exquisite wooden cradle having caught her attention.

"Isn't it beautiful?" she asked shyly, glancing at him and away again, biting her lip as if unsure whether she should have asked.

Jared's gaze moved from her to the cradle.

"Yes," he said, carefully schooling his expression to conceal his thoughts. Because regardless of the rules, he wasn't ready to talk about the baby, wasn't ready to make a decision regarding their situation. "My mother has saved our family cradle. It's five generations old."

He'd driven himself crazy this last week thinking about Lisa and the baby, and what part they would play in his life. If he'd learned anything from their estrangement, it was that he wasn't ready to walk away from his child. Twice he'd sent Zack to check on Lisa. Both times the report had been the same. Lisa radiated vitality and good health.

Jared, on the other hand, suffered from lack of sleep, loss of appetite and the inability to concentrate. Frustration had been building in him for days. Lisa had received the backlash of his pent-up emotions when she arrived on his doorstep this morning. And too much had happened since for him to know how he felt.

"That's nice. You're lucky to have family heirlooms, to have something of the past to pass on to future generations." Lisa watched the shutters fall into place behind Jared's eyes and reluctantly turned away from the window display.

If he'd been responsive, she would have told him how she'd been looking for just such a cradle to put in her studio so she could have the baby close to her while she worked. His withdrawal clearly indicted he didn't want to hear her plans.

In an effort to fend off her disappointment, she clasped her arm through his, bringing their bodies into intimate proximity, hard against soft. Niggling currents of sensation buzzed from every point of contact.

Desire pulsed like a living thing between them, its

existence refusing to be ignored. This morning's love play hadn't dulled the constant awareness. The attraction still sizzled, a breathing force, always present, always stimulating.

Conscious of their public surroundings, of the people passing behind them on the sidewalk, Lisa refrained from accepting the passion his blue eyes promised. She kissed him quickly, then stepped back a pace before the fire could ignite. With a shy smile, she swiped at the lipstick staining his lips.

He caught her hand in his, pressed a kiss into her palm. "Are you ready to go?"

"Yes." She turned and walked with him to the car. "Thank you for today. I'm glad we got a chance to spend some happy time together."

Jared opened the car door for her but momentarily blocked her way. "Have you been happy today?"

Lisa kissed his cheek. "You'll never know how special today has been for me."

He'd given her new memories, replacing the emotional for the clinical. For that she'd always be grateful. She couldn't tell him, not because he wouldn't understand, but because he'd understand too well. Then he'd be forced to face a connection between them he preferred to deny. Now wasn't the time to force the issue.

However, now that their day was over, she could share something close to her heart. "Let's go for a short drive. I want to show you something."

Jared followed her directions into the hills above Old Town until he pulled to a stop in front of a beautiful brick house with a lush green lawn and walkways bordered by roses. Watching Lisa watch the house, he saw the stars brightening her eyes, saw she had plans to buy the house.

"Ashley showed it to me. I've dreamed of living here with my baby. It's been on the market for months. The owners live in Europe. They're millionaires, or something, so they're in no hurry to sell. They can afford to wait until someone meets their selling price."

"They must want a mint, considering the location, the size and the view. The house will make a sound investment." Jared grudgingly gave his approval. It tore at his guts to hear her voice plans for the future, plans that included his child. But not him.

"This house will make a home," she said as if that was more important. "It's more than I can afford right now, but my paintings have been selling well. Maybe…well, never mind. I just wanted to show you. It's getting late, we better head for home."

Jared agreed. He needed to put distance between himself and the answers the future demanded. Like why did the best sex he'd ever had have to be with the woman pregnant with his child?

Back at his condo, Lisa climbed from the car and went around the back to join him. They walked across the garage to the elevators. When they entered the waiting elevator, Jared pushed the three button for his floor. Lisa reached around him and pushed the button for lobby.

"Why did you do that? You're coming upstairs with me."

"I don't think that's a good idea. I asked for the day and you gave it to me. Thank you. But I think it would be best if we end the day here. It's the logical thing to do."

Jared took her hand, raised her fingers to his mouth and kissed each individual knuckle, then he lowered her hand to cover his heart so she could feel the rapid beat of his blood. "My body doesn't know the meaning of logic," he said as he tugged her hand lower and pressed her cupped palm against the hard evidence of his desire.

The bell pinged, the doors began to open. He stopped them by pressing the close button.

"Jared." Lisa hesitated, unconsciously rubbing him through the denim of his jeans. "Are you sure?"

She was giving him the opportunity to stop what she'd started by asking for the day. He found he didn't want to end it.

"You asked for today. I gave it to you. Now I'm asking for tonight. What do you say?"

Without further protest, she stepped into his arms. "Three, please."

Chapter Eight

Lisa awoke to a light touch gently tracing over her still flat belly. She smiled sleepily, happy to wake with Jared beside her, to feel his hand over her growing child.

Jared's body faithfully molded itself to hers. The long length of his legs curved behind hers. His right arm fit the valley of her waist, and soft body hair tickled her in several sensitive places. His warm breath blew softly over her hair. And his hard maleness nestled intimately in the crevice of her bottom.

All things considered, she was more than content to stay right where she lay, unmoving and surrounded by the heat and comfort of her lover.

Lisa treasured each stroke of his hand. His careful touch told her, as nothing else could, of the depth of his feelings for the life they'd created between them.

Their child.

How easy the words came now that she loved Jared. She wondered how he referred to the baby in his own thoughts. He rarely used any designation at all when he spoke to her.

A particularly low sweep of his fingers caught her on an exquisitely sensitive patch of skin. Inner muscles clenched and released in reflex. The involuntary response activated an equally involuntary exclamation.

"Oh!"

"My God!" Jared sprang up onto his elbow, his hand splayed open over her. "Did you feel that? The baby moved. Isn't it early for that to happen?"

Lisa reached to gently cup his cheek. "That was me. You tickled."

"You're sure?" Disappointment replaced the fading excitement in his eyes.

"Yeah. I'm only three months along. The baby won't start to move until the fourth month. We have some time to wait yet."

"Oh."

His deflated tone nearly broke Lisa's heart. But he quickly shrugged off the mood. Desire darkened his eyes and lent a husky rasp to his voice.

"So, I tickled, huh?"

She nodded.

"And you clenched up tight like you do when I'm inside you?"

"Yes." She barely managed to breathe the word. His graphic description blazed through her system with only slightly less impact than the act itself.

"It drives me wild when you do that," he said. "When I'm so deep within you, and you're so tight and hot I feel I never want to move again. Then you'll do that little move, squeeze and clutch at me, drawing me deeper and deeper, urging me to move, driving me wild, giving me release. I feel like I'm in heaven on earth.''

"Jared." He painted a vivid, sensual picture of their mating. Her imaginative artist's mind easily inserted them into the scene.

"You feel it, too, don't you?" he said. "You're so responsive, so giving, it's a pleasure just looking at you. Your breasts are beautiful, plump and succulent.''

"You make me sound like a Thanksgiving turkey.''

Jared grinned. "No, more like peaches and cream." His hands roamed, investigating with intimate detail each of the areas he'd spoken of.

Lisa absorbed the sound of his voice, his touch, the words. All were equally erotic. She floated, lost to sensation, until he reached her femininity. His caress, though gentle, reawakened sore muscles.

"Ouch." Her body wanted, throbbed with need, but each pulsing surge set off a dull ache. Their bouts of lovemaking the day before had involved parts of her body unaccustomed to exercise. That, along with all the walking they'd done, made for some very stiff muscles in a very delicate place.

Jared hesitated, his body shielding hers. More than her exclamation caught his attention. He noticed her eyes, not the dazed look of desire, but the way they were narrowed in discomfort.

He felt her body tighten beneath his in anticipation, but also as if she was bracing herself.

With the lightest of touches he stroked her again, watching her face carefully for any show of distress. Because he guarded her expression so attentively, he saw the flinch she tried to deny. A warm rush of tenderness swept through him. She obviously hurt, yet she made no move to stop his advances. Her response nearly matched his in intensity.

"Are you okay?" he asked, his concern evident.

"I want you."

"I know. And you'd let me love you even when you're so tender each stroke would be agony. Our loving should always be a time of pleasure, never pain." He stroked his thumb along her cheekbone in a soft caress. "I know what you need."

Lisa fingered his chin, lifted her head and kissed him, at the same time cradling the hardened length of him in her other hand. "What about you?"

"I'll live." He returned her kiss swiftly then rose to stand by the bed, a magnificent, aroused male. "Don't move. I'll be back in a minute." He left the room, not bothering to stop for anything to cover his nakedness.

Lisa admired the graceful flex and flow of his form until he disappeared through the door. Pushing back the covers, she sat up, wincing. Balanced on the edge of the bed, she waited to see if her stomach would revolt. It didn't, she'd been incredibly lucky in that regard.

Jared's compassion touched her, though he credited her with more generosity than she possessed. When he touched her, all other considerations flew from her mind. Passion still pulsed through her system.

But he was right. She simply wasn't up to any sensual play.

"Lisss—a." Her name hissed between Jared's teeth as he reentered the room and caught sight of her perched naked on the side of his bed. He walked over to her, bent and gave each pouting, pink nipple a wet, spine-tingling kiss. "Come with me."

"Where are we going?"

He flashed her a searing look. "Paradise."

From the bedroom, her hand in his, they went down the hall into a room she hadn't seen before, which contained enough weight-training equipment to outfit a professional gym. Lisa silently thanked the heavens he didn't pause but went on into the next room.

More than a bathroom, this room held a walk-in shower, a sauna and, at the far end, a Jacuzzi. Steam rose to fog over the glass-enclosed area. Live green plants surrounded the sunken tub on the same three sides as the wall-length windows. Some of the plants hung from the skylight, others blossomed with fragrant exotic flowers, still more frilled out in lacy ferns. All were lush and well tended.

Lisa tensed, creating tension down the length of their arms. She didn't want to destroy the moment, but she hesitated entering the hot tub. Her doctor hadn't said anything, yet she'd heard and read things that indicated excessively hot water could be harmful to a woman in her condition. She made a mental note to address the question at her next appointment. In the meantime, she must be careful of the life she carried.

Her subtle stiffening alerted Jared to the potential problem.

"Don't worry," he said. "I turned down the heater last night. By now the water should be pleasantly warm. And I think you're early enough in the pregnancy the whirlpool action won't hurt you."

He didn't release Lisa but led her into the frothing water, descending the steps until the water lapped at their waists. He sat down, maneuvering her around to sit on the tile between his thighs, her head resting back against his chest.

"How did you know? Ah—you've been reading

again." Lisa relaxed and sighed. "Bliss, sheer, unadulterated bliss."

"Hmm."

"This room is lovely, like a jungle pool."

"Hmm."

"Hey, it's a glassed-in balcony. Very clever."

"Hmm."

"Are you going to sleep back there?" she asked with a peek over her shoulder. "Not that I blame you, this is marvelous. I feel quite recuperated." She rubbed her bare bottom suggestively into his manhood.

"No."

She made a face. "No, you're not sleeping?"

"No, you're not recuperated."

"Maybe I need to be massaged from the inside out."

A chuckle rocked his rib cage, erupting in a hearty laugh. "Lady, you amaze me. You need to rest."

"But you don't. I hate to think of you hurting."

Jared took a deep breath and exhaled slowly. The woman could tempt a saint. He wasn't accustomed to denying his own needs, yet for once he was making an effort, and she fought him every step of the way. As if her mere presence weren't a temptation in itself. Just the smell of her, wildflowers and woman, added to the ache in his groin.

If he were to give in to his body's demands, he'd be pounding into her, fierce and fast, satisfying every urgent desire he possessed. But he had more self-control than an animal. He'd practice restraint if it killed him.

Though having her pressed against him with only the transparent barrier of water between them sent a bittersweet torment throbbing through him. The sensual torture persecuted his body just as the memory of their mating haunted his thoughts. She suited him so well— in bed.

Her lustful nature matched his, heat for heat, passion for passion. But more, her generosity of spirit touched him in other ways. She gave freely of herself, offering him balance and a sense of perspective.

Their compatibility flat out terrified him. He preferred to concentrate on the physical, to forget the closing trap that commitment demanded and think only of the harmony required to make love.

"Let me help you." Lisa drifted away and turned to face him. "There's more than one way to make love. Let me pleasure you."

"Lisa—" Her name was a growl of broken restraint. "I don't want to hurt you."

"You won't." She assured him, positive in her own mind that no act of passion involving Jared could be harmful. "Last night you used your mouth on me."

Jared closed his eyes, savoring the memory. A small smile tilted up the corner of his mouth. "You tasted so sweet."

Pleasure and a tinge of embarrassment burned Lisa's cheeks to a becoming pink. "Let me taste you," she said, her blush deepening at her boldness.

Jared's gut tightened, sending a warm rush of tenderness slowly through his chest. He cupped his palms around Lisa's head, his fingers threaded into her damp, water-darkened hair. His mouth lowered to hers. He gave her his lips, his tongue, his taste and received hers in return. When the kiss ended, he rested his forehead against hers.

"You'll taste me, but now isn't the time or place."

"But—"

"Shh." He pressed a finger to her luscious lips.

"You need the healing power of the water. Give me your hand."

Slowly, giving her plenty of time to change her mind, he drew her hand down his body until her fingers wrapped around him in a snug embrace.

"Yes!" A moan of gratified approval vibrated from Jared's throat, hissing through his teeth. "Yes. A little tighter, tighter. Just like that. Perfect."

Lisa watched his face as slick skin glided along slick skin. Head thrown back, eyes closed, shadowed jaw clenched tight, his features told a story of intense, raw hunger. He'd never looked better to her.

She liked his beard. The stubble lent him a disreputable air. But, more than anything, she cherished his unconscious surrender. He'd placed himself in her hands, then lost himself in the exquisite sensations she created. Physically, he trusted her.

Because he did, she wanted all the more to give to him. On her next downward stroke, she lowered her hand to explore the territories below.

Jared instinctively arched into the unexpected caress. For a moment only, he let her test this sensitive part of him, her fingers gently squeezing and releasing in an erotic pattern that sent his blood rushing. His heart raced. Breathing became difficult, harsh, erratic. He came closer and closer to—

"Enough." He pulled her hand up and out of the water, kissed the back, then lowered their clasped hands back into the bubbling spa.

This time Jared guided the rhythm, and Lisa let him. She applied the necessary sensual pressure to carve a look of undiluted lust upon his features. His response fulfilled her in ways she'd never dreamed of. Knowing she pleased him, knowing she satisfied him celebrated everything in her that was woman.

When he reached the peak of his release, she shared the intensity with him. She licked along the straining muscles in his neck. Her pulse echoed the wild beat of his, and the heat of his accelerated breathing bathed her bare skin. His jaw clenched and unclenched, flexing to a primitive rhythm all his own.

Moments later, Jared's tensed body slumped back into the water. Lisa snuggled against him, her head falling to rest on his damp shoulder. His arm, hooked around her neck, held her close. She relaxed into his embrace, holding him in unmoving contentment.

Jared finally spoke. "If we don't move soon, we're going to be as wrinkled as prunes."

"Hmm."

Jared grinned at her sleepy nonresponse. "How are you feeling?"

"Hmm."

"Lisa?"

"Marvelous. I feel great." She lifted her head and eyed him, a distinct twinkle lighting her golden gaze. "Fully recuperated."

He braced her face with his hands and kissed her once, hard and fast. "Lady—" he shook his head, his eyes laughing at her "—forget it."

Lisa attempted a pout, but all she got for her efforts was another grin and a playful nip at her lower lip.

"Let's get you out of here before you catch a chill." He surged to his feet, pulling her up with him.

Water rushed away from them, leaving their bodies exposed and damp. The sudden change in temperature caused Lisa to shiver and goose bumps to break out on her arms and legs. He pulled a large bath sheet from a warming rack and briskly rubbed her down. As soon as she was dry, he grabbed her hand and began the return route to the bedroom.

"Jared." Lisa enjoyed the cosseting but felt she had to protest. "You're still wet. We could have waited for you to dry yourself, or better yet, for me to dry you."

"I'm fine."

Inside his room, he left her standing beside the bed to cross the room and retrieve some clothes from the wardrobe. He dropped the sweats into a heap on the bed.

"Put these on, and I'll move your clothes over to the dryer." He started to move away. Lisa flipped her towel up and out, catching him around the neck. He turned to face her, an eyebrow raised in question.

"You've been very thoughtful." She stepped closer, secured the towel around his lean hips and stood on tiptoe to kiss first his cheek and then his lips. "Thank you for washing my clothes. Thank you for everything." Not waiting for an answer, knowing he'd be uncomfortable giving one, she turned and reached for the sweatpants.

He disappeared into the walk-in closet and reappeared a minute later dressed in a pair of jeans and an open red shirt. "You know where the hair dryer is. Come out when you're ready. I'll start breakfast."

The simple task of transferring Lisa's damp clothes to the dryer required little effort. In the kitchen, Jared began assembling ingredients for breakfast. He noticed he was low on salt and noted it on the running grocery list kept by his housekeeper, who came in daily except weekends.

A lively tune filled the spacious work area, but halted when Jared realized he was whistling. The merry sound shocked him, but it also felt right. Shrugging, he went back to work, picking up the tune where he'd left off.

A loud, insistent beeping sounded from the building intercom. Jared grabbed up a towel to dry his damp hands, swung around and thumbed the intercom button. "Yeah?"

"Good morning, Mr. Steele. Your mother is on her way up."

Jared cursed, an obscenity that did nothing to relieve his stress. "Thanks, Burton. Have her car brought back out front. She won't be staying long."

Tossing the towel onto the table, he headed for the front door. He needed to waylay his mother. She didn't know about the baby. And he meant it to stay that way. Until the situation between him and Lisa became more settled, he felt strongly the two women should not meet.

He opened the door just as his mother had her fist poised to knock.

"Jared. You startled me. Oh." Disappointment erased the smile from her familiar round face. "Are you leaving?"

As an out, it would work as well as any other. "Hi, Mom. Yeah. But I'll walk you to your car."

"Jared?" Lisa called from the hall behind him.

He cursed under his breath. What lousy timing. He was halfway through the door, his mother on one side, Lisa on the other. Just the situation he'd hoped to avoid.

"Are you leaving?" Lisa moved toward him, confusion behind her question. He saw the uncertainty in her eyes.

"Wait for me in the kitchen." He tried to delay the inevitable. "I'll be right there."

"Son?" The familial address spoken in his mom's mother voice meant trouble, placing him up against a rock.

"Is this your mother? Aren't you going to introduce us?" Lisa stepped forward again, squeezing him into a hard spot by smiling through the door at his mother.

"No." Before she could respond, he closed the door between them. But not before he saw the smile disappear, not before he saw the hurt replace it. Damn, he'd wanted to prevent that.

"You were extremely rude, Jared. I taught you better." Kate Steele showed her disapproval by turning her back on him and starting for the elevators.

"Mom, I'm sorry. And I'll apologize to my friend when I get back. But now wasn't the time for introductions." The elevator arrived, and he followed his mother inside.

"See that you do apologize. There's no excuse for such behavior." She scolded as only a mother knew how to scold, and he knew he'd also hurt her. So much for his good intentions.

"Why are you here, Mom?"

An uplifted hand patted dark, silver-streaked curls into place. "It's been too long since you've been out to the house."

"I phoned you on Thursday."

"That doesn't count." She dismissed his claim with a wave of her left hand, diamonds flashing from her wedding ring. "All we discussed was how I was feeling and what I'd been eating..."

Jared froze, the end of her sentence going unheard as he recalled a similar accusation from Lisa. After a moment, he shook off the discomfort as coincidence, and as such, insignificant.

"...having a small dinner party two weeks from Friday. I'd like you to be there."

"For your birthday? I have the Chicago trip. I'm not scheduled to be back until that Friday."

"You can make it, can't you? For me? The guests will be family for the most part. Joanne is going to let the children stay up late. We're going to make it a double celebration. My birthday and Penny's. It's hard to believe she'd going to be eight. I remember when she was born, she was such a tiny thing."

"Babies generally are, Mom."

"Ah-ah." Kate shook her finger at him. "You play the cynic for my benefit because you don't want to hear another lecture on settling down, getting married, having your own children. You don't really fool me. Not for a minute. You've always been a nurturer. You're fighting your own nature when you deny yourself a family."

"Mother."

"Don't worry," she reassured him. "I'm not going to start. I want my birthday to be a happy day for the family. You're to come and enjoy yourself."

"Does that mean no eligible young women will be invited?" Jared flashed his mother a knowing look as the elevator doors fell open. He placed a guiding hand under her elbow and walked with her toward the front doors.

A betraying blush stained her powder-dusted cheeks. "I only want what's best for you."

"Please, Mom." He stopped beside her car. "Trust me to know what's best for me."

"I would, dear." She turned to face him, stepping

close enough to caress his cheek. "But I'm not sure
you'll recognize her when you find her." Her attention
focused on something beyond his shoulder. "It doesn't
look like your friend is going to wait for an explanation."

"What?" Jared swung around to follow the direction
of her gaze. Lisa bore down on them, her stride fast,
her expression, when her eyes met his, furious.

"Mrs. Steele." Lisa offered her hand and said simply, "I'm Lisa Langdon, a friend of your son's."

"Good for you, dear." The older woman graciously
accepted her hand. "I applaud you. This boy of mine
needs to be put in his place every now and again. I'm
Kathryn Steele, my friends call me Kate."

Lisa inclined her head, conscious all the while of her
disreputable appearance in Jared's sweats. Conscious,
also, of Jared's silence and disapproval. She knew he
wasn't pleased she'd forced this meeting between herself and a member of his family.

Good. He deserved a little grief.

"Kate. It's nice to meet you."

"Mother, we don't want to keep you."

"I'm not in a hurry, dear." Unfazed by her son's
rude interruption, Kate Steele launched into a new subject. "Tell me, Lisa, where did you and Jared meet?"

A quick frown revealed Jared's displeasure with the
new topic of discussion.

Lisa ignored him. When she'd left his apartment, she
hadn't planned this confrontation. But, upon seeing
them standing by the curb, she'd decided she couldn't
let him get away with treating her as he had. As honestly as she could, being as evasive as possible, she
responded calmly, "We met through a mutual acquain-

tance. One of those things where we were both in the same place at the same time.''

''How nice.''

''No, not really,'' Jared denied.

''Jared!'' His mother showed her distress at his rudeness.

''I'm afraid he's right,'' Lisa said. ''We didn't hit it off too well.''

''But you're still seeing each other? How interesting.'' Kate Steele's tone turned speculative.

The frown deepened across Jared's forehead. ''No, it's not. You're reading more into this than there is, Mom. Let me open your door for you. You can tell me what you'd like for your birthday.''

She looked ready to demur, then apparently decided against it. With a graceful shrug, she extended a hand to Lisa. ''It's been nice meeting you, dear.''

''A pleasure meeting you, Kate.''

Lisa watched Jared escort his mother to the front of her car. Their voices faded with the distance, not that Lisa listened.

You're reading more into this than there is.

Jared's comment kept echoing in her mind, drawing her attention inward. It distressed her to hear him belittle their relationship.

She shouldn't let the words bother her, she knew, because he didn't believe they had a relationship. But the hurt wasn't so easily dismissed. If he thought his mother saw possibilities where none existed, what chance did Lisa's hidden hopes have?

None at all.

How could she have faith in the future when he'd rather close the door in her face than introduce her to his mother?

She remembered something Jared had said once about his reasons for choosing to have a child. He'd wanted to end his mother's continued efforts at match-making. Had he meant the hurtful statement to discourage any attempts of interference?

Maybe Lisa was being too sensitive. Maybe she shouldn't analyze every word, every sentence, for hidden meanings. Maybe she should take each day, each hour, each minute she had with Jared and live the time to the fullest.

Maybe she should just love him to the best of her ability and let the future take care of itself.

She wished that were possible, but their baby, a part of that future, deserved better from her. The baby's needs must come before her own, before Jared's. And her self-respect would not easily pardon his distrustful, offensive conduct.

"Was that necessary?" Jared asked after waving his mother off. His tone held more curiosity than demand.

"I thought so, yes."

"Why?"

"I think the more important question is why you didn't want us to meet."

"I just didn't think the timing was right." He wrapped his fingers around her elbow. "Let's talk about this upstairs."

She firmly removed her arm from his grasp. "I'm not going back upstairs."

"Lisa, please, I didn't mean for this to happen today. I didn't mean to hurt you."

"But you did, Jared. Never close a door in my face like that again."

"I'm sorry. Now, let's go upstairs."

"No." Lisa shook her head. "We should have

known we couldn't put off the world. I gave you an ultimatum yesterday. It still stands. Let me and the baby into your life or stay out of ours. Let me know what you decide.''

Chapter Nine

"Shore Side Gallery, Lisa Langdon speaking. May I help you?"

"Miss Langdon, as I live and breathe. And here I thought you'd dropped from the face of the earth."

Lisa grinned, abruptly realizing she'd needed to hear Ashley's voice. "You exaggerate."

"Ha. Deny, if you can, that there are two more days of dust on your furniture?"

Visions of her bungalow as she'd left it this morning flashed in Lisa's mind, along with the list of chores left undone over the weekend. "Guilty as charged."

"I thought so." Smugness sounded in her friend's voice. "Was it worth it?"

New thoughts filled Lisa's mind, all of Jared and the time they'd spent together, both the good and the bad. "Every inch of it."

"Lisa! How naughty of you."

"Ashley! I meant the dust." Lisa didn't feel up to rehashing the newest development in the continuing saga of her relationship with Jared. She knew Ashley would understand. "We went golfing on Saturday."

"I didn't know you knew how to golf."

"I didn't. I still don't. Jared tried to teach me, but honestly, I defy any woman to hit a tiny ball with a long stick when a strong, lean man is pressed along the full length of her back."

"Mmm, where do I sign up for lessons?"

Lisa laughed. "You'll have to find your own instructor."

"How possessive of you. Does he feel the same way?"

She closed her eyes, her hesitation brief. "No." Always honest with Ashley, she could be no less honest with herself.

Ashley recognized the effort it cost her. "Good girl. Keep your head, and you'll be okay. How did he react to your list of demands. Do you think he's ready to take you seriously now?"

"I think so." Again Lisa evaded a more involved answer. "What's up? Or did you call simply to give me a bad time about my dusting habits?"

Silence was her only response while Ashley assimilated the change in subject. Lisa held her breath, waiting, hoping Ashley would let the issue rest.

"Actually," Ashley finally drawled, "I called in my professional capacity as your agent."

"Sounds promising." Relief lent a lilting note to Lisa's reply. "What have you got for me? Another commission?"

"How would you like to be one-third of a three-person show in December?"

An exhibition. The very thought robbed Lisa of speech. As a career milestone, a show could not be matched. She'd always thought of it in terms of the future. To be offered one now...

And to be shown with only two other artists! If the gallery were of any size at all, it would require a multitude of paintings.

"Hello? Lisa? Are you there?" Ashley's voice held amusement, as if she could see Lisa's stunned expression and hear the frantic thoughts racing through her head.

"I'm here. Details, give me details. I can't believe it. What gallery? Who else will be showing? Why me? I'm due in January, do you think it'll be too—"

"Hold it. Let me get a word in edgewise, and I'll tell you all about it. First, it'll be right there at the Shore Side—"

"The Shore Side. Here? But..." Lisa trailed off. Everything was happening too fast. She didn't know what to think. She'd never dreamed she'd be invited to do a show. Mrs. Dumond was so meticulous about the artists she endorsed. When Lisa brought in her work, she'd hoped for some concrete advice, but this...this surpassed all her expectations.

"Lady, *you* are good. How many times do I have to tell you? Mrs. Dumond loved your stuff. She wants to inventory what you have on hand so we can put together an estimate of what we'll need. The exhibit will start out with a holiday bash on the first then run for the month of December."

"Hoping to attract the seasonal shoppers," Lisa thought aloud while trying to assemble her wits. An extended viewing for an untried artist was unheard of.

"Exactly. Georgia Ralphston is being approached

for her pastel still lifes, and Wade Bond has agreed to show his abstracts.''

Ralphston and Bond. Obviously Nina Dumond meant to present some of the best up-and-coming talent on the West Coast. Both artists were masterful at blending colors, one shading subtly, the other splashing boldly. Lisa felt flattered just to be considered a contemporary of the two.

Ashley went on, continuing to outline the details of the event. Lisa made herself listen and absorb. Excitement at the offer bubbled within her, but underlying the thrill a vague sense of misgiving grew. She knew the amount of work required for a production of this size. Once she would have welcomed it, now she wondered what effect the undertaking would have on her unborn child.

"Stop," Lisa demanded. "I need time to think."

"Okay," Ashley accepted with a good-natured rebuke, "but don't take too long." They'd been friends far too long for her to be surprised by habitual caution on Lisa's part.

After disconnecting the call, Lisa sat for a moment staring into space. She had things to consider, decisions to make. And, she acknowledged, she'd like Jared to be involved in both.

She needed to think, but her emotions were too near the surface. It would be better, much better, for her to concentrate on work until her seething thoughts settled. Pen in hand, she focused on the column of figures waiting to be tallied.

"Lisa?"

Lisa started violently at the sound of her name. Pink cheeks betrayed the guilt of preoccupation when she swung to face her co-worker Rene. Beside her stood Kate Steele.

"Mrs. Steele." Surprised, Lisa rose to meet Jared's mother.

"Lisa, dear, I hope you don't mind me dropping by like this. Jared...uh..." Flustered, her words trailed off. She cleared her throat and glanced around the room, obviously uncertain about what she wanted to say.

"Please, come in." Lisa moved to her side. "Would you care for some coffee or tea?" She led her unexpected guest to the employee lounge.

"No, thank you. I won't stay but a moment. Jared—" She stopped then began again. "I want to personally invite you to a small get-together I'm having in a couple of weeks."

"Mrs. Steele, I don't know what to say." Lisa couldn't think clearly. This visit came too soon on top of Ashley's news. It was simply too much. Her nerves were raw, her instincts shot.

"Please, call me Kate. You must be busy. I shouldn't have bothered you here, but I thought it best to let you know about the arrangements I've made." She perched nervously on the edge of the overstuffed sofa.

Lisa sat down across from Kate. She felt more than a little frazzled herself. "What arrangements would that be?"

"For my birthday party. Both my daughters will be there, and Jared, of course. It'll probably be the last time we'll all be together for a while, with Paul and Joanne moving to Tokyo. At least I'll have next week with them. The sale of their house finalizes this weekend, so they'll be staying with me. I'll miss the children so, especially Penny. She's such a lovely little girl, so dainty, but with the mischief of the devil. She adores Jared, and he her.''

"He's very good with the children," Lisa said, a little concerned by the older woman's rambling. Kate seemed to be talking more to herself than to Lisa.

The observation about Jared earned her an odd look from his mother. A look that held elements of speculation, and, oddly, hope. The look disappeared when Kate smiled, suddenly serene. "You probably know Jared is leaving for Chicago next week. He won't be back until the day of the party, so I thought I'd send my car to pick you up, and Jared can give you a ride home."

"Kate, that's not necessary. I can drive myself."

"I insist. Dinner is at seven, so I'll have my driver stop by your place at six. Don't worry, I have the address."

Lisa gave in gracefully. She was finally beginning to realize the significance of this visit. As a sign of Jared's intent, it spoke volumes.

"I'm so glad everything is settled." Kate rose to her feet. "I have to go. I'll see you in a couple of weeks."

"I'll walk you to your car."

"Thank you, dear, no. I've taken up enough of your time. Take care of yourself."

Lisa sank back in the chair and watched Kate Steele make her exit. A slow smile lifted the corners of her mouth. Jared's quick response to her ultimatum pleased her. He cared. What better proof could she demand than the acceptance of her introduction to his family?

An hour ago her expectations for the future had been dim. Now the prospect held promise. Her career, the baby, Jared, everything was going to be all right.

* * *

"I can't believe I let you drag me miniature golfing." Jared carefully gauged the distance, looked down and softly tapped the ball. The yellow ball rolled forward, up, over, hit the embankment, rebounded and stopped within inches of the hole.

"Oh ho, Mr. Hole-in-one. Tell me you're not having a good time. And you're the one who wanted to practice his putting." A knowing look in laughing amber eyes dared Jared to deny his obvious enjoyment of the evening.

"Do you know how long it's been since I've done this?" He stood back and assessed Lisa's approach to the ball. She showed a marked disregard for all his instructions.

"You also said I needed fresh air and exercise. And you were right. I feel great, except I'm starving. Where are Ashley and Zack with the food?"

"They're probably fighting over who is going to carry what back to whom." Jared sank his next putt and wrote down his score of two. Three strokes later, he listed Lisa's score of four.

"The air fairly crackles between them, doesn't it? Let's let a few people play through until they get here. We're already two holes ahead of them."

"Okay. There's a bench behind you."

Lisa turned and saw the seat he'd indicated. She fished a rumpled napkin from her pocket and dusted the concrete before sitting down.

Jared watched, amused by her ministrations. "I was surprised when you called this morning."

She looked at him and smiled, a tender, delicate smile. "It wouldn't be fair to make you crawl."

A playful breeze lifted blond curls and blew them

across Lisa's forehead. Jared swept them gently back into place. He liked her. Too much. Especially when she made their difficult situation easy for him by changing her mind about forcing an ultimatum. Because he knew how much this meant to her, he graciously accepted her decision.

Besides, he had another subject he'd like to address. "Tell me something. Why did you invite Ashley tonight?"

"She came by earlier tonight, and when she heard we were going out, she sort of invited herself along. I think she wants to vet you," Lisa teased lightly then waited for his response.

One dark eyebrow slanted up, but the humor never left his eyes. "So, how do you think I'm doing?"

"Honestly?"

"Of course."

She sent him an arch look. "I don't think she's half noticed you."

Jared laughed aloud. "I bet you're right. Between fighting with Zack and feeding you subtle tidbits about the upcoming exhibition, I hardly rate a sideways glance."

"Here they come." Lisa caught sight of Ashley's striking red jumpsuit next to Zack's large, black-clad form. She watched affectionately as they began to wind their way back through the maze of storybook golf holes. "She's been remarkably restrained, actually. About my indecisiveness, I mean. She knows how excited I am to be offered an exhibition, yet she understands my need to put the baby first. It's almost as hard for her as it is for me."

Lisa returned her curious gaze to Jared's face. His profile, strong and shadowed, angled toward her. She wondered what he was thinking as he watched the return of their friends. Most of all, she wanted to know how he felt about her doing the show. She'd given him all the details, but they hadn't discussed her decision. And he hadn't volunteered his thoughts.

Now was a fine time for him to decide to respect her privacy.

His opinion had become very important to her. She glanced over to gauge the progress of the other couple. They were much closer. Now wasn't the time, but she needed to know what he thought.

"What do you think? Should I do the exhibition?"

Intent blue eyes swung to study her. She tried to control her features, tried to hide her anxiety, though she suspected her feelings leaked through.

The look in his eyes softened. "I think you're a sensible person. That you have the flexibility, determination and dedication required to do a good job. And I think you have the welfare of your child at heart to help keep everything in perspective."

Tears sprang to Lisa's eyes. She blinked several times to clear them away. Biting the insides of her lower lip, she sought composure. She'd never loved him more than in this minute when he offered faith and encouragement unconditionally.

"Thank you. I needed that." The husky words barely squeezed past the constriction in her throat.

"Don't you dare cry," he said. Her emotional response to a few words of approval astonished him. Then again, why should it? He knew she had few people in her life she felt she could talk to about this. Ashley, her closest friend, couldn't be the impartial, supportive sounding board she usually portrayed.

"I wouldn't dream of it." She smiled through the

conspicuous wetness, lifting a finger to collect the moisture gathering in the corner of her eye.

Jared shook his head at the obvious lie. Stepping up to the bench, he flung one long leg over it to sit astraddle, Lisa framed within the spread of his thighs. He pulled a handkerchief from a back pocket.

"Of course not, bright eyes." He handed her the cloth.

Lisa used the cotton square to dry her eyes and blow her nose, then she pushed the soiled handkerchief into her back pocket. "I'll wash this for you." She tilted her head to face him, offering a tentative smile.

He placed a lean finger against her full lips. "Don't thank me." They were so close Jared had only to incline his head for their mouths to meet. He made the necessary move.

He meant the kiss to be brief, a simple gesture of comfort and reassurance. The change came with the exaggerated rumble of two throats being cleared. Ashley and Zack were back. Jared's grin bared his teeth to Lisa before he deepened the kiss with a bold thrust of his tongue.

From there his intentions went astray. He wanted to provoke Zack and Ashley by prolonging the embrace. That's how it started. That's where it would have ended but for the unique, sweet taste of Lisa. As always, her essence drew him in, and he found himself sipping passionately from the intoxicating well of her luscious mouth.

He experienced the familiar rush of hot blood steaming through his system. Arousal came fast and hard, making the fit of his pants uncomfortable. He pulled back until a fraction of space separated them, and looked into her face. Then bent and claimed her mouth again with his.

"Ahhmm!" Bass and soprano harmonized as Zack and Ashley sought to make their audience status known.

"Do you think we should leave and come back?"

"I told you we had time to wait for the pizza."

"I didn't want to wait. I missed lunch."

Jared ignored the mild bickering. Something much more important was being revealed to him. Lisa loved him. He'd seen the emotion reflected in the depths of her golden eyes, the caring in the tenderness of her expression. For a moment he felt whole, complete for the first time in his life.

Joy flooded his being.

He possessed Lisa's love.

Panic followed close behind the happiness. Innocents died in the name of love. Best he remember the lessons of the past and protect his child against the illusion of romantic love.

With that thought he broke off the kiss.

"At last," Ashley stated in an aside to Zack. "I knew they had to breathe soon."

"You have no romance in your soul."

"I've no romance? Who's been throwing popcorn at them for the last five minutes?"

"If they want to eat, I figure they'll break it up before it's all gone."

"But the popcorn was mine."

The inane conversation never penetrated Jared's concentration. Much as he wanted to retreat, Lisa's vulnerability made him pause. He couldn't do it. He couldn't shatter her unsuspecting contentment with his customary icy withdrawal. It may cost him, tear at his guts every step of the way, but he'd create the essential distance by inches this time. He wouldn't be responsible for her first lesson in love being as brutal as his had been.

"Come on, come on, break it up. A pregnant lady needs her nourishment." Ashley barged forward and plopped a hot dog in Lisa's lap.

Jared raised narrowed eyes to study the other woman. She had his full attention now. Her belligerent expression almost dared him to deny her allegation. He met her stare for stare, neither acknowledging nor ignoring her.

Finally, he turned to Zack. "Why don't you and Ashley make up the holes you missed. Lisa and I will sit here and eat."

"I don't mind missing a few holes. I'll stay and eat with you." Ashley perched on the edge of the bench next to Lisa.

Jared exchanged a meaningful male glance with Zack. The large man hooked a strong hand around a fragile elbow and helped Ashley, none too gently, to her feet. "Come on, dynamite, let's sink some putts."

"I don't want— *ouch.* Unhand me, you big lug." Wiggling and protesting, Ashley ungraciously made her exit with Zack.

Unwrapping her hot dog, Lisa watched them go. "I'm sorry. She's very protective of me."

"I can respect that."

"You didn't have to send them away." Lisa took a bite and offered one to Jared.

He shook his head. "Ashley had nothing to do with it. You may not have noticed, but I'm in no condition to resume playing."

Seated within the open expanse of his thighs, her hip

crowded into his manhood, she was abruptly reminded of the truth behind his statement. "Oh."

"Oh?" An indecent leer accompanied the suggestive taunt. "Is that all you have to say?"

"What else can I say? I can't exactly do anything about it here." She shifted and settled, leaving a couple of inches between them.

"Spoilsport."

"Sex maniac." Again she wormed away from him.

His lean hand gripped high on the inside of her thigh, stopping further progress. "Where do you think you're going?"

Lisa caught her breath. Electric vibrations shot along sensitive nerve endings and collected mere inches from where his warm hand held her in a vise. "Not a smart move, lover." She removed his hand from her leg and linked her fingers with his to compensate.

"No? If you move much more, I'll be giving the kiddies a lesson in sex education."

Lisa blushed. In an unconsciously sensual act, she brought their joined hands to her mouth and licked a dollop of mustard from her finger. "At this rate, we'll never cool down."

Jared came close to groaning his agreement. The warm caress of her breath against his palm sent a tremor of desire straight to his groin. He savored her admission of arousal. He liked the way she shared the burden of their combined, if ill-timed, passion. Her honesty—

No, admiring her would get him nowhere. He was supposed to be deactivating their relat—acquaintance-ship, not furthering it.

"You, too?" he said. "Good. Why should I be the only one to suffer?"

"Selfish sexist."

They looked at each other in stunned silence before they both burst into laughter. Jared's new resolution slipped away.

Lisa shook her head in rueful denial and reached to tuck back a wayward lock of Jared's hair. "We're getting to be as bad as Ashley and Zack."

"God forbid."

"I'm afraid Ashley was rather vocal about our situation."

He waved her concern aside. "Zack knows."

Lisa bit her lip, unsure how to take his nonchalant attitude. She decided to be encouraged, to see it as a sign of his newly established commitment to her and their child.

"Good." She hesitated. "Why is he here?"

"I don't need anyone to protect me, if that's what you mean. He's here to make up the numbers."

"That's all?" She looked down. The hot-dog wrapper had been crumpled into a small ball. "He knows so much about me."

"Does he make you uncomfortable? You needn't worry. He's a fair man, and more than a little sympathetic to your cause," Jared's soft tone and easy manner reassured.

"Three." A defensive note edged Ashley's voice as it floated to Lisa on the warm evening air.

"Four," Zack argued.

"Ah, speak of the devils, here they come," Jared whispered into her ear.

"Three."

"Four."

"You don't count the stroke if you miss the ball."

"Sure you do."

"In professional golf, maybe. This is miniature golf, for children and fun. I don't suppose you remember— Oh, forget it. Add the stroke if it makes you happy." Ashley pasted on a bright smile as she approached the seated couple. "Hi, folks. Ready to move on?"

"Actually, I have to make a trip to the ladies' room," Lisa said. "You guys go on. I'll catch up." As Lisa passed Ashley, she entreated, "Behave yourself."

"I'll walk with you." Jared started forward, but found a slim, red-tipped hand planted firmly on his chest.

"No. Zack has to go. Don't you, Zack?" Ashley shot her current sparring partner a serious, beseeching look.

Too well trained to exhibit surprise at such a request, Zack looked to Jared for guidance. Receiving an acquiescent nod, he bowed to the bid for privacy, and turning with Lisa, moved with her toward the rest rooms.

"I'm sure you have a reason for instigating—"

"Please, Jared," Ashley said. "We're not in a boardroom now." She dropped her hand and retreated a step.

Jared watched her carefully, waiting for her to come to the point. Because she was important to Lisa, he'd listen to what she had to say.

"I want you to know Lisa's not alone in the world. She has someone who cares about her. I understand you're in an unusual situation and there are no easy rules to follow. But let me tell you something about the woman you're involved with here. Lisa is special. She's kind, and giving, and honest.

"We met under the worst possible circumstances. We were both in a foster home, she was eleven and I was nine. Even after a year, she hadn't learned to protect herself. I was born knowing. I tried to teach her not to care about the families, the babies, the other children. It only hurt when you were taken away, if you allowed yourself to become attached."

Mentally, Jared braced himself. He should have known when she cornered him that he wasn't going to like what he heard. That this independent, self-contained, beautiful and successful woman chose to expose herself in such a painful way was a tribute to the woman she spoke of, as well as to the unique bond of friendship they shared.

"She's a strong woman," Jared said.

"Yes, she is. She taught me more than I taught her. I couldn't stop her from caring, from giving of herself, but she became more selective. And I...I learned the true meaning of family. I love her. This baby means the world to her. You've made her happy, happier than I've seen her in years. If you hurt her, you'll have to deal with me."

Dr. Wilcox pulled forward a stool on rollers and sat with prim authority. She regarded Lisa with a serious, expectant look.

"Exactly what is your concern, Lisa?"

Lisa was at the doctor's for her regular monthly exam. She sat on the side of the examination table still dressed in a backless hospital gown.

"I just want to be sure, if I decide to participate in the gallery opening, that I won't be jeopardizing the health of my baby."

The doctor studied her through thoughtful, caring eyes. "I'll be blunt, Lisa. You're right to be concerned. With your history of uterine cysts, you have to be very careful. To your body, the pregnancy is a form of stress in itself. You must avoid any added stress to your system.''

Lisa stared at the doctor, dazed by what she heard. She felt fine, a little sleepy on occasion, but otherwise she felt wonderful. All thoughts of the show aside, she couldn't believe her baby was in danger because of her.

''Already I'm going to tell you to sit rather than stand, recline rather than sit, stay off your feet as much as possible.''

''I don't understand, Dr. Wilcox. I haven't felt bad, and I've done everything you've told me.''

''I know. And having issued my warning, I'll say this, you're in good health and you know your body better than anyone else. The show is obviously important to you. If you feel you can handle it without over-exerting yourself, then I'm not going to say you can't.''

''So you think it's all right?''

Dr. Wilcox shook her head, the gesture not unkind. ''Only you can answer that. I will remind you that you have another five and a half months to go and the strain to your system will become more pronounced. My advice is to listen to your body. And to avoid stress.''

''She says I have to avoid stress, that I have to stay off my feet.'' With Ashley, Lisa didn't try to hide her dismay. Her friend would understand the dilemma she confronted. Two lifelong dreams, two elements of her life that she loved to her soul—her child and her painting—and to reach for one put the other at risk.

''Oh, Lisa.'' Ashley settled on the white leather sofa in her ultramodern condo and gave Lisa a hug. ''Is the baby all right?''

''Yes.'' Touched, Lisa laid her head on Ashley's

shoulder, grateful for the concern for both her and the baby. "And I'm fine too. But the cysts have weakened my system, and I have to be extra careful."

"You're worried about whether you should do the show?" Ashley cut right to the heart of Lisa's anxiety.

"It's going to be a lot of work. If I start to feel bad or Dr. Wilcox puts me on complete bed rest, it wouldn't be fair to Mrs. Dumond for me to pull out at the last minute."

"Lisa, you can count on me to support you in whatever you decide. And I know you, you'd never do anything to jeopardize your child, so that's a nonissue. If you want to do the show, I'm here to help. And from doing the inventory, I can tell you, you have enough paintings to show without lifting a paintbrush between then and now. It doesn't have to be a stressful event."

"I'll worry. You know I'll worry."

"You'll be excited and anxious over your success, but there'll be no need to worry. I'll take care of everything."

"You're too good to me." Lisa squeezed Ashley's hand. "I can't let you put your life on hold for me."

"You aren't *letting* me do anything, I'm offering. And it wouldn't be putting my life on hold. I also have an interest in seeing you succeed."

Lisa looked at her friend and lifted an eyebrow. "Don't try to tell me the commission you get off my paintings is anywhere near what you get when you sell a house. I won't believe you."

Ashley met her arch look with a serious gaze, making Lisa sorry she'd mentioned money. She knew Ashley only meant to show her support. The thing was, Lisa didn't know what to do. She wanted to go for it, to do the show, but she felt guilty for wanting it, even knowing Ashley would be there to help.

"I'm sorry," Lisa said.

"I understand. This isn't easy for you. I'm just saying I'll be there for you whatever you decide."

"That means a lot to me, you mean a lot to me. Thanks."

Jared stood, hands in pockets, in the department store and watched Lisa turn her feet one way and then the other. "I think I'll get this pair. What do you think?"

He thought she looked good in whatever she wore. The strappy green sandals did do nice things for her pretty feet with their red-tipped toes. "I like them."

"Good. I'll get them." Sitting on one of the department chairs, she slipped off the shoes. "Can you pay for them while I put my running shoes back on?" She reached into her purse then handed him her wallet.

Jared carried the shoes and her wallet to the cashier, but paid with his own charge card. He wanted to do this small thing for her though he knew she'd fight him if she knew. He was pocketing his wallet when she joined him at the counter.

"Look at these." She held up tiny hightops no more than three inches long. "Aren't they cute?"

He looked at the shoes, then at Lisa and decided to humor her. "Yeah, they're cute, for doll shoes."

She grinned at him and shook her head. "These aren't toys, they're baby Reeboks."

"You're joking."

"No, they're real. Aren't they adorable? And look at these." In the palm of her other hand Lisa cupped a pair of booties with bows. "Aren't they darling?"

They were even smaller than the baby tennies. He nearly choked at the thought of handling a being small enough to wear such microscopic shoes. But at the same time, a sense of wonder at what he'd created began to break through the shell he used to protect himself.

"Jared? Are you all right? You've gone white."

"I think I need some air."

Concern chased the smile from her face. She set the shoes on the counter, and when she turned back to him, a knowing look lightened her eyes. "I know what you need. Come with me."

She hooked her arm through his and led him down the aisle to the baby department.

He instinctively hung back at the sight of the miniature clothing and baby paraphernalia. He'd rather brave the lingerie department. At least there he knew what things were and where they were worn. From where he stood, he had doubts about several items in this part of the store. Was that green thing a hat or something to cover the baby's bottom?

Lisa faced him, issuing a dare with the cocky tilt of her head and a lift of her eyebrows. "Come on, Daddy. Think of it as another test."

Oh, she knew how to get him where it counted. He couldn't resist the challenge. Neither could he let her get away with it.

"I'm going to get you for this."

"Promises, promises." She laughed and tugged him forward.

The happy sound lightened his mood, and as he moved through the racks of infant wear he began to get into the spirit of things. The green thing turned out to be a cap with matching shoes.

"Everything's so tiny." Dresses, shirts, pants, even the pajama-bag things, which he didn't really understand. "How does the kid get his feet loose?"

Lisa gave him a strange look and said, "He doesn't, that's the point."

Huh.

Lisa practically danced her way around the racks, showing him this, admiring that, oohing and aahing over each little thing. Her joy brought out a new beauty in her. She glowed, and he realized the illumination came from inside, from maternal pride and a soul-deep love for her child. The realization stirred both hope and fear. Opposing emotions he didn't know how to deal with. So he ignored them both and simply enjoyed the moment.

They compared strollers, high chairs, bathtubs and cribs, discussing color choices and decorating themes. He liked the gold and blue of moon and stars, she liked the bold green and soft turquoise of dolphins and whales.

Babies were everywhere he looked. A laughing toddler wanting to walk and holding on to mom's hand. A redheaded little sweetheart cuddled in her father's arms. And a set of twins only three weeks old asleep in a double stroller. Lisa stopped to admire and chat, but Jared made his escape.

The thought of two babies made his knees shake.

In all his research, how had he missed the fact that babies were so small. Best he get used to the idea now, because in a few months he'd be holding his own baby in his arms.

Turning into the next aisle, he found himself faced with a baffling assortment of bottles, nipples and breast pumps. In bottles alone he saw plastic, glass and disposable, short and tall, straight and angled, and more. Nipples were just as varied and even more complicated. He could choose from round, nubbed or orthodontic, but that wasn't all. He still had to choose between slow flow, fast flow, safety or self-adjusting.

"Hey." Lisa caught up with him, and placing her hand on the small of his back, rubbed back and forth. "What are you doing?"

He gestured to the selection in front of him. "How are you supposed to know which to use?"

She surveyed the assortment then shrugged. "I plan to breast-feed the baby."

Jared simply stared at her, completely undone by the thought.

He should have known that would be her choice, should have been prepared for the thought of his child nursing at her breast. But he hadn't allowed himself to think beyond the moment.

From the beginning, he'd planned to hire a nanny to handle the baby's care. Yet only last night he'd read the chapter on baby feedings and realized what that entailed. A feeding every one and a half to three hours throughout the day and night for the first six weeks and sometimes longer.

How could a stranger, an employee, be expected to handle such a schedule? Even with relief and his help, the responsibility might be too much without an emotional bond to offset the physical demand.

He knew now he didn't want a stranger raising his child.

He'd been so sure he could do this alone. And he'd have made the situation work. He'd have hired the kindest caregivers, filled the nursery with the highest-quality baby furniture, bought top-of-the-line strollers and car seats.

The baby would have lacked for nothing.

Except for a mother's love.

"Jared?" Lisa demanded his attention. "Say something."

He looked at her, saw the beauty and goodness of her, recognized a woman who hadn't hired her body out as a surrogate, but who already loved and cherished the life growing within her. And he knew he couldn't put off the future any longer.

He forced a half smile. "We have to talk."

"Ouch. From the look on your face, that hurt." Her smile matched the gentleness in her eyes, in her touch.

He didn't smile, he couldn't. Catching her right hand in his, he held it clasped against his chest. "We haven't really discussed what we're going to do about the baby. This—" he squeezed her hand to show he meant the physical intimacy between them "—isn't an answer."

"No," she agreed, her tone soft as a whisper. "But it could be part of the answer."

That surprised him. He met her gaze and the expression in hers hadn't changed. Gentleness and understanding lightened the gold in her eyes. "How?"

"We've created a link between us that will never go away. I don't know what the future holds, but we now have a past. We've been building a foundation. And that's a gift we can both give our child."

"So that's how you see our relationship, as a gift to our baby?" He didn't know how he felt about that, but something made her smile brighter than the fluorescent lights overhead. "What?"

She lifted her eyebrows at him, making no effort to stifle her grin. "You said the R-word."

Her irrepressible spirit made him want to laugh. Instead, he pulled her close and lightly nipped her bottom lip with his teeth. "You're not going to let me be serious here, are you?"

"No." She lifted their clasped hands and bit the pad of his thumb with delicate, white teeth. "We have time. Let's just work on our gift for a while."

Lisa stood behind Jared, watching his reflection go through his usual grooming routine as he got ready for his trip to Chicago.

His behavior lately kept her constantly guessing. Everything would be going great, with long stretches of intimacy and closeness, then, for no apparent reason, his mood would swing. He hadn't exactly fallen into his former cold attitude, but something was wrong.

Whenever he made love to her, it was with a ravishing tenderness that communicated a poignant desperation. Almost as if he thought each time they came together might be the last.

Yet, from amorous affection he'd switch to being casually aloof. He was withdrawing, subtly, more mentally than physically, but withdrawing all the same. It upset her that the incidents were happening more and more often.

She so much wanted to talk to him about her decision regarding the show, but anytime she mentioned anything to do with the future, he'd change the subject. And it hurt.

Because he mattered, because their future depended upon it, she persisted.

And she welcomed each small victory. He didn't want her to drive him to the airport, but she was determined.

"There's no need to call a cab. I can drive you."

His gaze met hers in the mirror then he glanced away. "It'd be a wasted trip for you."

She moved around him to wedge herself between him and the dresser. Taking the trailing ends of his tie, she knotted it for him. "No time I spend with you is wasted."

She won that round. He drove her car to the airport, and though he again protested, she had him park and went into the terminal with him to see him off.

At the gate, she turned to him. "Have a good trip."

"Take care of yourself while I'm gone."

"I will. I'll even take notes of what I eat so you can review them when you get back."

He arched a dark eyebrow. "You're naughty, you know that."

Despite all his objections, his farewell kiss held all the heated vehemence she might hope for.

Jared threaded his fingers deep into the glossy length of Lisa's hair, cupped her head in his hand and pulled her face to his. Softly, his mouth melded to hers. Immediately, she opened for him, inviting his possession. He delayed a full invasion, lingering to sip attentively at her lips. He gave with all of himself, his tender touch massaging her nape, the subtle stroke of his tongue, teasing in its retreat, bold in its forward thrust.

The world ceased to exist around her. She heard only the beat of her heart, and his. The public-address announcements, the shrieks of welcome, the cries of farewell made no impression.

In an infinitely precious caress, he trailed his free hand down her arm to entwine his fingers with hers. Slowly, they surfaced from the passionate interlude, ending the kiss once, twice, three times before finally separating. As a farewell, the embrace far outdid simple words.

Lisa licked her lips, hoping the gesture would help to settle her surging senses. It didn't work. She tasted him, with each flick of her tongue she gathered the lingering essence of him. She repeated the motion, which defeated her purpose as Jared captured the provocative sweep in midlick.

This kiss held none of the gentleness of its predecessor. It was hard and quick and touched her to the center of her heart, and loins.

"Goodbye." His voice held a husky rasp, and again she felt a shiver vibrate to her core.

"I..." Undone, Lisa tried to clear her throat. "I uh...call me."

A knock sounded at Lisa's door. She gave her loose curls one last, nervous fluff. Moments later, she sat in the back seat of a luxurious vehicle.

Apprehension regarding the coming party filled her mind. She wished she knew better where things stood between her and Jared.

He hadn't called, not once.

Given his odd behavior before he left, she feared he meant the separation between them to be permanent. At least physically.

"Miss?"

Lisa started and snapped her head around. The driver stood beside her open door. She gathered her things and the gifts and stepped from the car.

"Thank you." She offered the man a smile.

"My pleasure, Miss Langdon."

Wide oak doors swung open to reveal Kate Steele.

Her flowing caftan suited her perfectly, just as she suited the traditional ocean-view estate.

"Lisa, I'm glad you could make it. I'd like to talk to you, but first come in. I'll introduce you to everyone. Jared should be here shortly."

An uneasy tingle raced up Lisa's spine. Something didn't feel right. Jared should be with her the first time she met his family.

Going through the introductions, seeing the varying reactions to her presence, did little to reassure her. She followed Zack, a familiar face, thank heavens, to the bar, where she accepted a glass of iced cider.

As she sipped, she looked around the room. Jared's two sisters, Joanne and Mary, occupied an antique sofa, his brother-in-law, Paul, stood propped against the marble mantel. Kate had run to the kitchen to check on dinner. The children, David and Penny, played on the Persian carpet at their mother's feet.

She looked at Zack. "No other guests are coming, are they?"

He shook his head. "Just Jared."

Lisa's sense of dread deepened. "I'm surprised he agreed to my being invited."

Zack came from behind the bar to join her. "Did he?"

"No." The answer came from behind her. And, shockingly, the disclaimer came from Kate Steele. "That's what I wanted to talk to you about."

Lisa was allowed no opportunity to comprehend the importance of her revelation.

"Uncle Jared! Uncle Jared! What did you bring me?" Pigtails bouncing, Penny streaked across the room to throw herself into her uncle's arms. "Your girlfriend is here. Are you going to marry her? Grandma says you are.''

Lisa's heart sank as tension tightened its grasp on her. Even from the far side of the room, she saw the accusation blazing at her from arctic blue eyes.

Chapter Ten

The sharpness of Jared's piercing glance sliced through Lisa, and she knew in that moment she should never have come here tonight.

He worked his way through the room, stopping to greet each member of the family. Deceptively pleasant, he kissed first Joanne's then Mary's cheeks and shook hands with his brother-in-law. Only the heavy pitch of his voice belied his lighthearted manner.

He reminded her of a shark, slowly circling its prey.

As a true measure of his affection for his family, he managed to camouflage his rage for their benefit. He might deny it, he did deny it, but he was a family man at heart.

Lisa stared, fascinated, as he approached her. Amazing how alert yet wary a hunted creature could be. She found she couldn't move. She waited, helpless to evade him.

"Mother." He greeted the older woman with a kiss, not noticing the paleness of her complexion, ignoring her attempt to speak to him.

"Zack," he acknowledged his friend.

"Jared."

"And Lisa." At last he reached her side. The look in his eyes condemned. The harshness carved into his features intimidated. "I missed you." The words, the sentiment were correct, but his tone made a mockery of them.

He bowed his head, enshrouding her. The hard line of his lips mashed unto hers. Roughly, his tongue invaded her mouth to ravish. The softer elements of a kiss were missing. No tenderness, no gentleness, nothing to seduce the senses. He meant to punish and he succeeded.

When he lifted his head, Lisa felt bruised, humiliated in front of his family. Abruptly, he turned his back on her and walked away.

Shock, she thought. She must be suffering the effects of shock to stand and take such treatment.

"I'd like to leave." Lisa addressed Kate Steele without taking her eyes off Jared's retreating shoulders. "Please ask your driver to drive me home."

Silence greeted her request, then a weak-voiced response. "I can't. It's his night off. He left after he dropped you here."

This news took a serious toll on Lisa's vitality. When she swung to face her hostess, her eyes were empty of expression. "Couldn't you even leave me a means of escape?"

What color remained in Kate's cheeks drained away at Lisa's challenge. She gained no satisfaction from the older woman's distress. Neither could she forgive the interference in her life.

"Would you please call me a cab?" Lisa requested quietly.

Panic sprang into Kate's eyes. "Please stay. I don't want my daughters to know what a mess I've made of things." Her worried gaze moved from Lisa to her daughters and back to Lisa. "Please."

A strange wave of resignation settled over Lisa. Reluctantly she nodded. For whatever reason, it seemed she was meant to play this through. So she chose a seat, sat back and, with morbid fascination, watched the events unfold before her.

A few minutes later, the dinner bell rang. She found Kate's none-too-subtle matchmaking extended to the dining table. Lisa's designated place had her sitting next to Jared. She drew a fortifying breath into her lungs and pulled out her chair. Would the night never end?

Both she and Jared participated in the conversation, though he carefully refrained from speaking directly to her. Seated next to him, she absorbed the hostility emanating from him. His left hand remained fisted throughout the whole meal.

"Lisa? Would you care for anything more?"

She looked up from a dismal contemplation of her plate. Forcing a smile, she politely refused Joanne's offer. For once, Lisa's healthy appetite had deserted her.

"What should we do next?" Kate asked Penny. "Ice cream and cake or presents?"

"Presents!" came Penny's enthusiastic reply.

"Ice cream! Ice cream!" Two-year-old David chanted his preference.

"Okay, we can have cake first." Already the peacemaker, Penny succumbed to her brother's demand. The cake, a lavish affair of roses and happy wishes, brought an excited gleam to the little girl's eyes. "Make a wish, Grandma, then we'll blow the candles out together."

"A wish?" Kate sent a futile glance in the direction of Jared and Lisa.

Her eyes didn't quite meet Lisa's. Obviously the evening, so carefully planned, wasn't turning out as Kate had intended. Lisa almost felt sorry for her. Almost, but she'd discovered the charity in her heart didn't extend to that degree. Not tonight. Maybe not ever.

Wishes were made and the candles blown out. Joanne sliced the cake. Lisa's stomach revolted at the sight of the sweet concoction. She swallowed convulsively and her smile faltered.

"Eat up," Jared whispered against her ear, his anger breathing over her. "This is a birthday party you got yourself invited to," he said harshly.

Instead of warmth, she felt a suffocating chill at his nearness. She sent him a quelling glare. His direct attack caused a crack to form in the numbness surrounding her. What was with him anyway? Okay, he hadn't known she'd been invited, but he must realize she was just as much a pawn in his mother's scheme as he. When she thought—

No, better if she didn't think. Thinking came too close to feeling, and she couldn't allow that. Not here. Not now. Because, she very much feared, when she did begin to feel again, the pain would be unbearable.

"Time for presents." Penny hopped out of her chair and ran from the room. "Come on, everybody."

"No running," Paul called out, busy helping David

from the high chair. Tolerant adults followed the excited children at a more sedate pace.

Lisa stood to join the others.

Jared blocked her exit. His arm spanned the empty doorway while the bulk of his body rested against the frame. "Smile. This is a party not a funeral."

"Yes." Fed up and fighting off the beginnings of a headache, Lisa's pseudo calm came to an abrupt end. "I can tell by your festive mood."

"Don't get sarcastic with me. You wrangled yourself an invitation to this little get-together. If you're less than satisfied with your reception, you have only yourself to blame."

She shook her head. Blond curls rustled loose across her shoulders. For his benefit, she'd worn her hair down. She wondered why she'd bothered. "I didn't wrangle anything. Your mother invited me."

Jared fixed narrowed eyes on her. "Was that before or after you spoke to your lawyer about suing me for child support?"

A cold hand wrapped around Lisa's heart and squeezed. "Where did you hear that?"

"Where doesn't matter. I should have known your innocence was an act, that your willingness to 'share' custody was an attempt to extort money from me. And if that's not bad enough, you push your way into my family home."

"That's not true."

Jared put his face next to hers, close enough for her to smell the Scotch on his breath. "Honey, you wouldn't know the truth if it came up and spoke to you in the street."

"Enough, Jared. Yes, I saw a lawyer, an insensitive, money-grubbing, publicity-seeking shark of a lawyer.

I went to see him because this baby is too important to me not to know my legal position. I'm sure you know yours.''

Jared's eyes narrowed. Though he gave no verbal response, his silence acted as an admission of sorts and as testimony of his control. Obviously, he didn't want to give anything away by speaking in anger.

Lisa's chin lifted a notch. ''Don't you get it? The joke's on me, not you. I thought you'd arranged this. I'd asked you to make a decision about our situation. Stupid me, I believed the invitation came from you. I thought you'd sent your mother to invite me as a token of your acceptance of us, the baby and me.''

He waved a dismissive hand. ''When you called me the next evening, I figured you'd had the intelligence to rethink such an idiotic ultimatum.''

Her back went up in affronted dignity. ''It was not an idiotic ultimatum. My life turned upside down with the confirmation of this pregnancy. I don't know my own body anymore. My appetite is erratic, my hormones are worse, and I burst into tears for no reason at all. I can't even trust my moods because my emotions are beyond my control. How dare you dismiss my request as idiotic, when all I wanted was an assurance of consistency from you?''

''There's a vast difference between commitment and consistency.''

''I wasn't asking for a commitment to me but to the situation. Was it really too much to ask for a little consideration and certainty from you?''

He ignored her question as if it had never been spoken. He didn't have an answer, which forced him on the defensive. Anger and resentment overrode reasoning.

He eyed her three-piece pastel pantsuit. The camisole top, cut in a low V, exposed a tantalizing view of her increased cleavage. He knew how tender her breasts were, how soft to the touch. He sneered, resenting the contrary urge to tell her how lovely she looked, smelled, felt. His loins hardened in familiar, traitorous desire, a reminder that her appeal for him was strictly physical.

"At least you had the decency to wear something that conceals your condition."

Lisa looked into the face of the man she loved and felt empty. "You're despicable."

She cared for him so much, but he gave her only suspicion and mistrust in return. She saw the hunger his eyes couldn't hide, but his desire meant less than nothing when no softer emotions were there to back up the passion.

His comment regarding her clothes cut along raw nerves. Now four months pregnant, the new changes in her normally slender body thrilled yet confused her. Her reactions ranged from awe to despair. His attitude belittled those fragile feelings. Especially as she'd consciously chosen to wear a suit styled on loose, flowing lines. Not in a shamed attempt to disguise her pregnancy, but out of respect for Jared.

Kate hadn't mentioned the baby on her visit to the gallery, so Lisa had assumed Jared hadn't told his mother. He had the right to inform his family of his impending fatherhood in his own way, in his own time. He deserved that courtesy.

He did not have the right to insult her integrity or her appearance.

"How can you say that to me? After the time we've

spent together, is that all you've learned about me—that I'm a lying, manipulative frump?''

Again silence greeted her question. A silence accompanied by a blank blue gaze that spoke louder than mere words.

''I see,'' she said. Infuriated, Lisa lowered her head. She took a deliberate step backward. His hand dropped from the doorjamb to his side. ''I wonder why you've continued to see me.'' She straightened her spine, angled her chin and lifted her gaze to meet his dark, fathomless eyes. ''Good sex? If that's all there is between us, then there's nothing between us at all. There's no need for us to see each other again.''

''You don't mean that.'' His quick frown hinted at second thoughts.

Lisa was beyond caring. She wanted away from him, far away. ''I do. Please move.'' The thought of touching him, even the casual brush of their bodies in passing, was intolerable.

''You can't just end it like this.'' He crowded her, his tone a cross between threat and entreaty. ''There's more involved here than sex.''

''I used to think so. Now I realize it was wishful thinking.''

''The baby is still a part of both of us. You can't just walk away from the situation.''

''You walked away first, when you didn't respond to my request for a commitment.'' She squirmed past him, managing by a concentrated effort on her part, to avoid physical contact.

Every instinct she possessed urged her to put time and space between herself and the man who so callously dismissed her needs. She wanted to go home, but she had no car. She entered the front salon, and after scanning the room, approached Zack to ask for a ride home.

Jared followed her into the room, but at Penny's request went upstairs to assist Joanne with the nightly tucking-in rituals.

"Poor Lisa," Zack sympathized. "You haven't had much fun tonight, have you?"

Lisa bit her lip and glanced around the room at Jared's relatives. "It's been a long time since I've been part of a family gathering." She shrugged. "Maybe it's a dream I'm not meant to live."

"You don't mean that."

"No." She treated him to a wan smile. "But right now I really need to go home. Do you mind taking me?"

"Lisa." Kate joined them by the fireplace. "I'm going to have Paul drive you home. I don't want Jared driving tonight."

"He's only had two drinks, Kate." Lisa couldn't help protesting on Jared's behalf, though she immediately told herself to stay out of family business.

"It isn't just the two drinks. I haven't seen him so upset since his father passed away. I'm sorry for the trouble I've caused."

Zack sipped his club soda. "You only want what's best for Jared. But he's a man. He has to make his own choices."

"This discussion is getting us nowhere," Paul interjected from the couch. "What we need to decide is who's going to drive Jared home." He paused, hesitant to continue. "And how we're going to get him to agree."

"I'll ask him to stay the night here," Kate said.

"Mom." Mary's gray eyes blazed behind sooty

lashes. The sudden, stunning resemblance between her and her brother caused Lisa to catch her breath. "You know he'll refuse. I hate it when reminders of Beth show up like this. It's ridiculous. I can't even offer my own brother a ride home because of some witch from his past."

That caught Lisa's attention. Who was Beth? And what part did she play in Jared's past?

"Mary," Kate protested mildly, casting a sidelong glance toward Lisa.

"I'm sorry, Mom, but there's no other word accurate enough to describe her." Mary stood and paced, ignorant of her mother's subtle reminder of Lisa's presence. Energy crackled around her. "We never talk about her, and we should. You remember how she was, especially about his car. Always asking if she could drive, racing around in it as if she owned it, as if she owned him. And he let her because he loved her. Now he thinks if he gives up his keys, he's giving up control of his life. It's just not right."

"Right or not, we have to respect his feelings. Maybe he'll consent to riding home with me," Zack volunteered.

Lisa listened to the interchange with mixed emotions. Beth must be the woman Jared had spoken about. His former fiancée. So, now she had a name to go with his past. But, she reminded herself, the information meant nothing to her.

It came too late.

"I like Lisa, Uncle Jared." Penny's arms hugged Jared's neck in a sleepy hug. "You should marry her like Grandma says."

Sometimes Grandma talks too much, Jared thought.

"You'll always be my best girl," he said, tapping his niece's nose affectionately before bending to tuck her into the bedding and kiss her good-night.

"Me, too. Me, too." David held up his arms, demanding Jared's attention from the adjoining twin bed where his mother had settled him. When he and Joanne traded places, he bent to bury his nose in the sensitive curve of David's neck. The boy giggled, his small hands clutching Jared's hair, and at one point, his ear. As most babies did, he smelled of soap and powder and love.

"Good night, Davie." Jared kissed the toddler's soft cheek and stroked his blond curls until he calmed enough to sleep. Quietly, Jared followed Joanne from the room. They slipped into the hall, half closing the door behind them.

"Precious, aren't they?" Joanne whispered.

Jared nodded, preoccupied. Holding his nephew had reminded him of his responsibility to his own child, which in turn helped him regain a sense of perspective. He'd made a mistake, a big mistake. One he might not be able to backpedal fast enough to get out of.

"I don't know if I like your friend as much as Penny does. What did Lisa do to upset Mom?" Joanne's comment intruded on Jared's self-recriminations.

"Leave it alone. It's more complicated than you know."

"This is Mother's birthday, she shouldn't be made to feel—"

"Joanne." Jared shot a stay-out-of-it look at his sister. He didn't want to have to defend Lisa to a member of his family. He didn't need any reminders of his brutal conduct.

"Okay." Joanne held up a hand in surrender. "It's

your business, but mind it, brother, because I won't stand by and watch Mother get hurt." With that said, she hooked her arm through his and walked with him downstairs. "Now, tell me, how did you get your hands on Disney's newest release? I know it doesn't open in the theaters until next week."

"I have my sources," Jared said, leading her into the salon.

"I just bet you do." Joanne released him to snuggle into the corner of the couch with her husband. She lifted Paul's arm to slip under it, her fingers linking with his. "The kids are safely tucked away."

"Mother." Jared leaned over the chair where Kate sat. His hands curved around her upper arms, he brushed her powder-scented cheek with his. "I'm going home. Good night."

Kate caught his hand in one of hers. "Jared, please, you aren't thinking of driving? Zack has said he'll see you home."

"That's not necessary, Mom." Jared came to an impromptu decision. "Lisa can drive me home."

Lisa downshifted Jared's Mercedes, wincing when the gears protested loudly. She glanced over at him. He stared out the window at the continuing, passing darkness, showing no response at the harsh treatment of his expensive car.

Why had he wanted her to drive? She asked herself the question for the tenth time in as many minutes, her attention once again on the traffic. More to the point, why had she agreed? Being alone with him could only mean added pain and mental distress.

Stress, just what the doctor warned her against.

Of course, she knew why she was there. It had been

emotional blackmail, pure and simple. The hopeful stares of his astounded family had silenced her objections almost before they formed. And after hearing the revealing family discussion, how could she possibly justify refusing him?

"I'm not drunk."

The stillness inside the vehicle ended with Jared's quietly spoken, clearly enunciated statement.

"I know." Lisa didn't doubt him for a minute. To give himself over to drink would mean surrendering his precious control. Which only made his concession as a passenger all the more puzzling.

"I'm sorry."

Lisa heard his apology but refused to respond. The words were too easy to say.

When she'd anticipated seeing him tonight, she'd planned on throwing herself into his arms and devouring him with deep, hungry kisses. She'd missed him so much.

Instead, their first physical contact in days had been a rough, punishing kiss.

The evening had been a complete disaster. They'd been linked by invisible cords of awareness yet distanced by solid barriers of suspicion.

"We need to talk."

At his statement, something clenched tight in her stomach. It frightened her, the hope that flared inside the despair. She wanted to say no. Logic told her to say no. Only the remorse hidden in his deep voice caused her to hesitate. Several miles sped by while she warred within herself for a reply.

"I think we've said all there is to say between us," she finally said, unable to give any other answer, wishing all the while it could be different, knowing it could never be. He'd betrayed her when she was too vulnerable.

Now she needed to heed her doctor's advice and think of her child.

He looked at her once then returned his gaze to the window. They traveled the rest of the trip in silence.

Lisa used the time to prepare for the painful experience of saying goodbye to Jared. After tonight, she wouldn't be seeing him again.

He had demons to put to rest, and until he did, there was no hope for them as a family. From this instant forward, she needed to think of her child first, no more living for herself. Because Jared couldn't look beyond the past, she must be the one to take on the responsibility of the future.

She pulled to a stop in Jared's underground parking space. He got out, but Lisa sat still for a minute, putting off the future for as long as possible.

He came around and opened her door. She had no choice but to climb from the car. She did so without looking at him. Her heartbeat quickened. The sense of dread, constant throughout the evening, intensified to the point of excruciating torture.

They stood, careful not to touch, waiting for the elevator. She watched the floor indicator display the descending numbers. Seconds ticked by, bringing the end of their relationship ever closer. Maybe, she thought miserably, she should just say goodbye and take the stairs to the lobby, where she intended calling a cab.

The doors swished open. She stepped inside followed by Jared. Then experienced an undeniable flash of familiarity when she reached to press the lobby button and he stopped her.

"Please." Closing her eyes, she begged softly. It

was both a prayer and a protest. But, when she opened her eyes, she still saw, and felt, Jared's hand holding hers suspended above the buttons. Her attention focused on his wrist, on the broad gold band encircling it, on the near-transparent hairs curling over it, on the deceptive strength hidden within it. "Let me go."

"Come upstairs," he said. "I want to explain."

Blond strands of her hair caught on the textured lapels of his jacket as she shook her head. "No."

"Please."

To hear him plead was her undoing. Tears blurred her vision until the sight of their hands became indistinct. "What good will it do?"

"Just listen to me. Give me a chance to make you understand."

If he hadn't been touching her, she'd find denying him easier, but his hand cupped her shoulder, his face played over her hair and his heat enveloped her.

"I'll listen." How could she refuse the explanations she'd waited so long to hear? "But sometimes understanding isn't enough."

Chapter Eleven

The silence in Jared's shadowed living room neared deafening proportions. Lisa sat on the couch staring into a darkened corner. An internal debate waged inside her head as she prayed she'd made the right decision. It was so hard to know what to do, what was for the best. She could only hope understanding would provide some answers.

He'd chosen to sit at her feet. She couldn't say why. The broad stretch of his shoulders rose above the edge of the couch supporting his back. An inch of shared body heat separated them. Jared had deliberately established the physical space between them.

Lisa compulsively swept her hand across the plush gray velour of the seat cushion. The soft texture tickled her palm. The action failed to appease the desire to run her fingers through his dark hair. She longed to touch him, to feel the vital strands cling to her hand as she soothed them both with caressing strokes. But she dared not breach his self-inflicted isolation.

She, too, needed the distance.

Every minute that ticked by seemed an eternity. Why didn't he speak? Did he regret inviting her in, or was he simply having trouble assembling words?

When he spoke, his voice was low, distant. "I met Beth during my last year at college. She was so beautiful I think I fell in love with her the first time I saw her.

"I couldn't believe my luck when she returned my feelings," he continued in a toneless voice. "We got engaged. Nick had been my best buddy since high school. He and Beth didn't get along real well. I never suspected—not for a minute—that they were having an affair."

Lisa heard the pain vibrating below the surface of his memories and wished she held a better view of his face. She despaired at his choice in sitting turned away from her.

"To make a sordid story short, the engagement was a con. Beth planned to marry me, stay for a year, divorce me, then she and Nick would live happily on the proceeds of community property and alimony. I found out about the scheme and ended it."

But not, Lisa could tell, before the betrayal of friend and lover devastated him.

Jared gave a derisive, self-mocking laugh. "The next thing I knew, I was being summoned to court on a paternity charge."

Lisa caught her breath. "She got pregnant?"

He angled his head toward her. "She swore it was my baby," he said over his shoulder. "I was always careful about birth control, I want you to know that.

But Beth had a plan and a soul corrupt enough to use an innocent babe to achieve it. I had to believe her. At least until tests could be done.''

Compassion for a younger, vulnerable Jared consumed her. He'd been faced with the prospect of fatherhood and the scandal of a trial while still suffering from a double betrayal.

No wonder he found it hard to trust. No wonder he needed to be in control.

Wanting to comfort, Lisa slid to sit on the floor beside him, effectively breaking through the barricade of pride, his and hers. She curled her feet under her, rested her head on his shoulder and entwined both arms around one of his.

''What happened?''

He shrugged. ''I went to see Beth. She gloated openly. Told me of the plans she and Nick were making for my money. She didn't boast for long.'' His voice hardened. ''I told her I was countersuing for custody, and she wouldn't get a penny.''

Lisa flinched at his blunt claim. Blood raced through her veins. Sweat broke out on her palms. Her world spun as, for one horrible fragment of time, it was her child being threatened.

Almost immediately her universe righted itself. Jared would never do anything to deliberately hurt any child. He would, however, do whatever he thought necessary to protect that child.

''What did Beth do?''

Even in profile she saw the anguish wash over him. He closed his eyes and his jaw tightened. His Adam's apple bobbed as he swallowed hard. ''She told me— no money, no baby. I called her bluff, had her served with custody papers." He paused, fought for control. "She killed the baby."

The words rocked through Lisa, stealing her breath. "My God."

"She had an abortion. No money, no baby."

"How awful." Lisa wrapped her arms around his neck, hugging him, offering comfort. How he must have suffered. "Jared, I'm so sorry."

He turned to her, resting his forehead against hers. She felt his breath shudder through his body as he sought for peace within himself.

"How did your family react? You're so close."

"I never said anything to Mom or the girls," he said, his words empty of inflection. "Dad had just passed away. Mom survived a day at a time. Joanne was newly married herself, and Mary—poor kid—she had a rough senior year. Circumstances demanded she mature almost overnight."

"You must have been desperate."

"I was a romantic fool. I deserved what happened to me, but when Beth tried to victimize my family, particularly at a time when—" He cut himself off. Rehashing the past, especially this portion of his past, didn't come easily to him. Too many painful truths lay hidden in his subconscious. "I did what I thought was best."

Her gaze met his and Lisa saw beyond the sophisticated facade to the vulnerable man beneath.

"You needn't look like that." His gruff denial sounded near her ear. "I'm not about to take you to court. The risk...the pain...I can't live with that kind of emptiness again."

Her heart melted, as she realized he blamed himself. In a desperate bid to protect his family, he'd done what he deemed necessary. As a result, he lost his child. He thought he'd failed when in fact he'd done the best he could to protect everyone.

Beth was the one at fault, not Jared.

Today he required reassurance of that fact. She longed to give him the peace he craved. Yielding to his need and hers, she feathered his hair away from his creased forehead. Her fingers threaded through the healthy, dark mass, she rhythmically massaged the tension from the clenched muscles at the nape of his neck.

His inability to trust, his fear of commitment, were explained. Surviving a brutal lesson in deceit and betrayal when his heart already ached for the loss of his father had left emotional scars. It wasn't that he cared if someone drove his car, it was a matter of being in control so no one could ever destroy a part of him again.

She rested her head against his upper arm. Under her cheek, she felt the cool fabric of his shirtsleeve, and under the cloth, his strength. Hard. Tough. Strong. He was all of those and more. Yet he could be gentle, compassionate and remarkably selfless. His nearness alone gave her a sense of comfort she hadn't experienced since she was ten years old.

"What are we going to do about us, Jared?" she asked, the question a mere breath of sound.

He shook his head. "You don't understand. There is no us, there never can be."

She frowned, not quite following him. "What do you mean?"

"I can't trust myself. I let them get too close."

Lisa sat up. In amazement she turned to face him. "That's ridiculous."

"No, it's the truth."

"It's hogwash." A flip of her delicate hand dismissed his absurd notion. But when he looked at her and then away again, his wounded soul briefly reflected within the depths of his eyes, she realized he believed every word he said.

Urgency filled her. A compelling need to convince him he was wrong. "You've had relationships since then."

"Affairs." He stressed the word. "Nothing of any meaning."

Pain, fierce and demeaning, washed through her. She knew in his mind their involvement belonged in the casually discarded category. Only because the issue was so important did she continue her arguments. "There's your family."

"Family's different."

"What about Zack?" She sought desperately to find a positive example. "He's your friend."

Jared thought for a minute before nodding. "Zack's a friend, but we understand each other. He has his limits, and I have mine."

For the second time in the space of only a few hours, Lisa felt her future slipping through her fingers. He refused to look at her, so she scooted closer, cupped his jaw in her palms and waited until his gaze met hers. His blue eyes were glassy, almost glazed.

"Listen to me," she urged. "Have you any idea how astounding this sounds? You're in charge of an international company. You make decisions on hiring, firing, delegating and promoting based on people's qualifications and personalities, their characters. How can you possibly doubt your ability to judge a person's character when you do it on a daily basis?"

"Business is different."

"No. I'll accept family is different, but business isn't. The only distinction is trust."

"I've already said—"

"It doesn't wash, Jared. It's easier to blame yourself, but the truth is, you don't trust me."

"Not true," he denied, shaking off her touch. Then he shook his head. He was tired, and the alcohol he'd consumed earlier began to catch up with him.

"You're punishing yourself for no good reason," she insisted. "The past is gone, let it go. Don't let Beth and Nick deprive you of a future." She melted back into his lap, wrapped herself around him and dug her chin into the opening of his shirt. "Please," she begged him. "Don't let them prevent you from knowing your child."

His large frame rested on the carpet under hers. From the curve of her shoulder to the arch of her instep, she pressed against him. Each breath he took stirred loose wisps of her hair. She smelled the lingering scent of Scotch. Maybe he'd had more to drink than she thought.

Suddenly Lisa found herself crushed within his strong arms. He buried his face in her hair.

"I love my baby." The smothered declaration reached her in a voice so low she almost missed hearing him.

"I know," she whispered, tightening her arms around his waist. His confession sent a poignant rush of tenderness to warm her entire being. She swallowed hard in an effort to block the tears welling in her throat. How sad that such a strong man should fear love.

They sat together in the dimness of the room. A light trailing in from the hall broke the darkness. Neither Lisa nor Jared spoke. They simply touched. It was enough for the moment, this quiet awareness of each other. Questions and answers were forgotten while their spirits communicated.

After a few minutes, his crushing embrace eased, then he gently set her aside and rolled unsteadily to his feet.

"I need a drink." His hands ran over the wrinkled front of his shirt, patting the various places his jacket pockets normally covered. "I need a cigarette." His gaze searched the room as if he expected the items to suddenly materialize.

Lisa got to her feet. Obviously, today's travel and tonight's indulgences were catching up with nim. She took him by the hand and led him down the hall. "You don't need anything more to drink, and you don't smoke."

"Oh." He accepted the news easily enough, easier than she accepted the end of their conversation. "Where are you taking me?" Jared ran a hand over his face then the back of his neck, the gesture characterizing his weariness.

"To bed."

"To bed?" When they entered his bedroom and he saw the bed with its inviting fullness, his tone turned hopeful. "Are we going to make love?"

"No."

"No?"

"No."

"Then why are you undressing me?"

Lisa bowed her head to hide a bittersweet smile. He stood before her, passive as a child, while she unbuttoned his shirt, but his mind and body were all male. "I'm putting you to bed."

"But not to make love?" At the negative shake of her head, he asked, "Why not?"

She lifted her gaze from where her fingers worked at his belt buckle and met intense blue eyes clouded with genuine puzzlement. His right hand rose to her head, and he played softly with her silky blond hair. "I like making love with you. Better than with anyone else."

"We can't." She barely managed a whisper as she fought to control her overwhelming response to him. He touched her, and bones she'd never had trouble with melted to mush.

"Why not?" he asked again.

She gritted her teeth in frustration. Life was not fair. If it were, he wouldn't be standing there forcing her to fight him as well as herself. Fortunately, he was fast running out of steam.

"We don't know each other well enough." Despite the times they'd made love before, tonight had taught her the painful truth. Much to her sorrow.

"Sure we do." He offered no resistance when she gave him a soft shove so he sat on the bed. She went to work on his shoes and socks. "You're Jared, I'm Lisa...and we made a baby together."

A sharp bounce of the bed caused her to look up from her crouched position. Jared lay flat on his back, arms flung out to the sides, his eyes hidden beneath lowered lashes. Totally vulnerable and, as always, emotionally inaccessible.

"You could at least have helped with the pants." She spoke half to herself and half to the sleeping figure.

One eye blinked open to look at her, then the other followed. Lisa held her breath. She hadn't meant for him to hear, to respond. But he had, and rather than ignore her and fall peacefully back to sleep, he struggled to his feet. His less-than-accurate fingers fumbled at the buckle on his belt until he realized it had already been undone. The zipper proved easier. He pushed silk pants and blue briefs down and off. His shirt joined the growing pile of clothing forming at his feet.

Naked, he climbed between the sheets. An uplifted arm beckoned her to his side. "Come here."

Even as she stepped forward, she shook her head, torn between love and self-preservation. He had only to look at her, and her body began to ready itself for him. He had only to ask, and she gave. It would always be so, which wouldn't be bad if he loved her. But he didn't, and she knew, now, to hope would be futile.

She sank onto the bed next to him. Immediately, his arm encircled her neck, though he required no exertion to bring her mouth to his.

She needed to taste him as badly as she needed to draw her next breath. This kiss must last a lifetime. She sipped from his lips, memorizing all the different textures of his mouth, the unique, masculine flavor. His lazy, almost dreamy, participation suited the mood perfectly. She took her time, savoring every passing moment until she recognized his stillness.

He was asleep.

Tenderly she brushed the hair off his forehead. A dull snore sounded loud in the quiet room. One lone teardrop slid down Lisa's cheek. The dampness clung to her for an endless millisecond before falling to land on the hard curve of Jared's shoulder. She kissed the wetness away.

"Thank you for my baby," she whispered, her voice husky with controlled emotions. She pulled the covers up around him, then after one last look she walked away.

It hurt to lift his eyelids. He'd denied being drunk. He told himself he didn't have a hangover. But it hurt to open his eyes. Probably jet lag, he rationalized. That and the sunshine hitting him full in the face. An indication he'd slept well past his usual waking hour.

With a groan, Jared rolled to his back. Flashes of last evening's events rose to haunt him. He remembered the fury he'd experienced when he walked into his mother's salon and found Lisa chatting cozily with Zack. Past and present had collided, and the similarities seemed blatantly obvious.

He groaned anew when he thought of the shabby way he'd treated Lisa.

Unconsciously, he'd superimposed Beth's faults onto Lisa. It hadn't been until she questioned his knowledge of her in such a way as to threaten the end of their relationship, until he spent time with his sister putting his niece and nephew to bed, that he realized the damage he'd done.

He left the bed, chased away by the emptiness. If he were to lie still for another moment, he'd be admitting to himself how accustomed he'd become to her presence in his life. Something he wasn't prepared to do, not yet.

Running a lean hand tiredly over the stubble darkening his cheeks, he made his way to the bathroom. He showered and dressed before heading to the kitchen for a much-needed cup of coffee. And aspirin, at least two, extra strength.

He found the letter on the sink.

Propped against the coffeemaker. Impossible for him

to miss, as anyone who knew him would know. He never went without his morning cup of coffee. He filled his cup then sat down to read the letter.

He tore open the envelope, his gut clenching, anticipating a blow. The existence of the letter alone alerted him to the contents. Lisa was nothing if not direct, nothing if not honest. He'd lost sight of those facts for a while last night. Today, with her letter in his hands, he acknowledged the truth. Which could only mean trouble. He unfolded the piece of paper.

Dearest Jared,
Thank you for last night.

I know it wasn't easy for you to talk about your past, and I don't want you to think I didn't appreciate the effort it cost you. To know why things could never work out between us is better than always wondering about what might have been.

Our child will grow up knowing who his father is. Maybe, at some point in the future, we can discuss visitation rights. But for now, stay out of my life. Please.

I know that sounds harsh, but I have to think of our baby, of providing for him or her both emotionally and physically.

Knowing you physically has been one of the greatest joys of my life, but emotionally, you drain me. There's nothing left for myself, let alone for the baby.

Please give me time.

Love,
Lisa

Jared crushed the single sheet in his fist. Never

would he allow her to walk away while she carried his child. He reached for the phone, but abandoned the motion before he completed the action. When he confronted her, he didn't want the width of a major city between them. This needed to be handled face-to-face.

The figures refused to add up again. Lisa threw down her pen in disgust. She rubbed at the ache in the center of her forehead. The pain persisted, and she gave serious thought to going out at lunch and picking up some of the pain reliever sanctioned by her doctor.

"Lisa?"

At the sound of the familiar voice, her head became too heavy for her neck to support. It took every bit of strength she possessed to lift her head and look at Jared.

Anger vibrated from him as he stood framed by the doorway. The clatter of Rene's typewriter and the drone of Mrs. Dumond's voice from the next room faded into the background.

Why, Lisa asked herself, couldn't he have accepted her letter and let the matter end without another confrontation?

"What are you doing here?"

"I want to talk to you."

"Please. Go away. We've already had this discussion."

"Not this one we haven't," Jared denied. "Not the one where I agreed to let you take my child and walk out of my life."

Her awareness of the others abruptly returned. The sudden silence only intensified the need for privacy. Her dignity wrapped around her like a cloak, she retrieved her purse from a bottom drawer, tucked it under her arm and walked toward Jared.

"Rene, I'm going to lunch. I'll be back in an hour."

Outside she headed north on the shop-lined street. She watched every step, deliberately maintaining distance between herself and Jared.

"Well?" he finally demanded.

Exasperated by the need to go through this yet again, Lisa rounded on him. "Well what? Honestly, Jared, what do you suggest we do? We can't go on as we have been."

"So you said in your letter. I disagree, running away isn't going to solve anything."

"I'm not running, I'm facing facts. There is a difference."

"Not from where I'm standing. It looks like take the baby and run. I can't let that happen, Lisa. I can't lose another baby. I know it's the easy answer for you, but for me it's not an option."

"Easy?" she echoed in disbelief. She thought of the anguish, the sheer emotional turmoil that had gone into her decision. For him to casually dismiss those feelings hurt. It also reinforced her need for this separation.

"How can you say that to me? You know I was as much a victim of your mother's matchmaking scheme as you. Yet you treated me like…like…" She stuttered to a stop, too upset to properly voice her thoughts. "I have never been so insulted."

Head bowed, she turned to walk blindly forward. "There's no telling what your family must think. And all because of the false image you have of yourself."

"What are you talking about?"

"You say you can't trust your own judgment of others. Well, I say that's damn convenient. It's much simpler to shoulder the responsibility and the chip that goes with it than it is to place the blame where it belongs and get on with your life.''

''So, I should have blamed the other guy, shrugged off all personal involvement and gone on with my life as if nothing ever happened?''

''You're guilty of being young and in love, that's no great crime.''

Jared thrust his hands into his pockets. ''We should learn from our mistakes.''

Lisa glanced at him, then away, noting the stubborn set of his shoulders. It wasn't right. He'd done little to merit a life of loneliness. And she doubted her arguments were making any difference.

Though doing so left her feeling helpless, she needed to try one last time. ''It's time to forgive yourself.''

''It's not a question of forgiveness.'' He stared into the distance. ''It's a matter of survival.''

Lisa stopped and faced him. ''Then there's nothing more to say.''

''This is insane.'' Jared halted beside her. ''My past has nothing to do with the future.''

''I can't chance believing that.''

''Why not? You wanted to spend time together. I think we should go on as we have been.''

''No.'' Why did he have to make this so hard?

Lisa turned away, but not before Jared caught a glimpse of the despair shadowing her golden eyes. They strolled in silence. She scrutinized each shop window they came to with devoted intensity. How did he reach her? She was different today, cooler, less approachable than he'd ever known her to be.

He eyed the space between them, gauging it to be about eighteen inches, a foot and a half of physical emptiness. Emotionally they might as well be on opposite sides of the vast Pacific Ocean.

There had to be a way to melt her icy demeanor. If he were to crowd her, he'd be able to break through the barriers she'd erected to trace the delicate length of her neck. One touch and she'd be his. He knew the power he held over her. He knew, because she held the same power over him.

But he hesitated, disliking the thought of using passion as a tool. Then he considered the consequences of not reaching her at all. He saw the future, bleak and lonely, spread out before him. He imagined never seeing his child or Lisa again, and he bridged the distance between them in a single step.

With the back of his hand he swept aside a fall of her silky hair. He felt her shiver of awareness as the tips of his fingers encountered her sensitive skin. Pressing his advantage, he placed a kiss on her exposed nape.

"You said knowing me was one of the greatest joys of your life," he said.

"We can't spend all our time together in bed." Her response was a husky disclaimer.

"We can try."

"No." She tried to pull away, but he held her fast. "I can't."

"We're good together," he insisted. "You could move in with me." The invitation surprised even him. He inhaled a bracing breath, absorbing her familiar scent of wildflowers and woman. He waited for the panic to hit. Instead, he felt a curious sense of relief, of rightness.

For one brief, exultant moment Lisa rejoiced in his proposal. He offered more than she'd ever expected he would. The overture tempted her beyond belief. However, when the flash of longing passed, she acknowledged living with him wouldn't really resolve anything. It would only postpone the inevitable.

Because she loved, she wanted more. Because of the baby, she must demand more.

His offer touched her, touched her deeply. It couldn't have been easy for him to extend the invitation. Opening his home to her went against all his rigidly held, carefully built barriers. A tide of love rushed through her first warming, then chilling her. To reject him when he was at his most vulnerable—

It hurt her to think of hurting him. He'd never know how much.

The baby. If she kept their baby in the forefront of her mind, if she thought of the future in terms of their child's welfare, she'd be able to do what had to be done. Her doctor said no stress, and Lisa couldn't think of anything more stressful than trying to second-guess Jared.

She faced him with her decision. Regret clouded her eyes. "I'm sorry."

His blue eyes turned wintry, icy gray. His expression hardened. "Don't tease, Lisa."

She shook her head, slowly, sadly. "I'm sorry, Jared, I can't."

He released her, stepped away from her. "Can't? Or won't?"

"Both."

His scowl deepened. A war waged behind the frozen facade of his features. Lisa wished she knew what his thoughts were. Did he mean to accept her word and walk away, or would he continue to challenge her? She suffered a thousand uncertainties while she waited.

"Why?"

She'd dreaded the question. The decision had been difficult enough to make without having to explain it. They'd been over this again and again, and each time it got harder to hide her true feelings. She'd been as open with him as possible and still protect her pride.

At least she could give him part of the truth. "Because I've already made a commitment. To Mrs. Dumond, to Ashley, and to myself to do the show." Tears burned at the back of her eyes. She swallowed hard before continuing. "Dr. Wilcox told me no stress. I agreed to go on with the show when things were going good between us. I plan to honor my commitment."

"So you're choosing your career over your child's father?" he challenged, his tone cold enough to freeze granite.

Pedestrians brushed by them on both sides. One man waited for his wife to pass before pushing a stroller around them. "Keep it moving," the man muttered in annoyance.

Jared slowly angled his head to look at the man. His expression never changed. Cold. Remote. Dangerous.

Immediately, the man held up a hand in a pacifying motion, shook his head to say he'd meant nothing by his comment, then, gathering his family together, he quickened their pace away from the couple blocking the sidewalk.

More than the question, the incident affected Lisa in a strange way. She remembered other times when they'd been interrupted. The teenagers on the beach, his employees, the children, each time he'd handled the disturbances with patience and courtesy.

During the give-and-take of their tenuous relationship, she'd learned a few things about him. Rarely was he intentionally rude. Of course, he possessed vices. He could be relentless, even ruthless, but he was also caring, sensitive, generous. And, she scolded herself, if she weren't careful, she'd talk herself into giving in to him.

Only the fear of a future shadowed by his constant doubts helped her keep her resolve. Nonetheless, she realized, she owed him the explanation he'd requested. If she balked at sacrificing her pride, she need only think of what she wanted of him.

She'd ask him to relinquish a part of himself into her care. He'd be making a far larger sacrifice than she.

He waited silently, demanding a response.

"I can handle the show, Jared. I can't handle you." Lisa inhaled a deep fortifying breath then said the words clearly and with proud emphasis. "I love you with all my heart, with all my soul."

He blinked once in astonishment. The expressionless mask he wore cracked, shifted, remolded itself into a semblance of wariness. The intensity of his gaze made her feel as though a tight band were wrapped around her chest, squeezing until she lost the ability to breathe.

"That sounds more like a reason to agree." The chill in his voice matched the look in his eyes.

"I want to. More than anything, I'd like to come live with you, love you, be a family with you. But I can't."

"Damn it. Why not?"

"Because I refuse to spend my life catering to Nick and Beth. I'd lose all self-respect if I did."

"I'm not asking you to—"

"Yes. You are. You don't mean to, I understand it's not intentional, but look at last night. You didn't plan on treating me like a liar and an outcast. It was pure reaction. Whether the source stems from lack of trust in yourself or in me doesn't matter. What matters is the trust isn't there." The last sentence barely qualified as a whisper.

"We can build on what we have."

"What do we have? Without trust there's nothing between us but lust and the baby. And I won't, I absolutely refuse to subject him or her to a life of suspicion and unrequited love. Our child is innocent of any blame in this situation. Our baby doesn't deserve to suffer for our mistakes."

Lisa met his gaze straight-on. Because she knew what she asked of him, she let her love shine through. "I know you're afraid of losing another baby, but that's not what's happening here. I just need time. Please," she begged in earnest. "Let me nurture our child in peace."

For a long moment he stood with his gaze focused on something over her left shoulder, avoiding direct eye contact. Finally, reluctantly, he conceded.

"All right. You have my word. I'll leave you alone." When his eyes did meet hers, a terrible pain dulled the usual brilliant depths. "But only until the baby is born."

Chapter Twelve

After signing her name, Lisa reread the letter she'd just written. She'd said more than she'd wanted to in some places, as in asking Jared to make peace with his mother. Kate had called Lisa earlier in the week and invited her to lunch. Lisa had had to decline. At six months she was definitely showing and she didn't think Jared had told his family about the baby. Lisa was pretty sure Kate would have said something if she'd known.

And she'd written less in some places than she could have. She'd downplayed Dr. Wilcox's warning of a possible cesarean by playing up her anxiety in starting her Lamaze class and Ashley's nervousness at being her coach.

The rest of the letter discussed possible name choices for the baby. For a girl, Lisa liked Samantha Kathryn after their mothers. For a boy, she was less decided. Her father's name, Frederick, she felt was too old-fashioned. She wished she knew Jared's father's name.

Biting her lip, she eyed the closing and thought about changing it, but decided not to for two reasons. She did love and miss Jared.

And because he'd never read the letter.

Opening the top left-hand drawer of her desk, she carefully placed the three new pages on top of the stack of letters, all pink, all addressed to Jared, all unmailed.

She needed the outlet for her feelings. It was important for her to be able to share this time in her life with the father of her child. So she wrote her thoughts in the letters but never mailed them.

"There you are." Ashley spoke from the doorway. "I knocked. When you didn't answer, I got worried and used my key to let myself in."

Lisa smiled at her friend. "I hadn't realized before what a worrywart you are."

"You've never been pregnant before," Ashley said defensively. "Are you ready to inventory your stuff?"

"I'm ready when you are." Lisa awkwardly pushed away from the desk, forgetting as she did so to close the drawer containing the letters. "You'll be proud of me. I didn't lift a finger to get started before you got here. It was tough, but I managed to restrain myself."

Jared pushed open the front door of his apartment. Then, dropping the keys into his pocket with one hand, he used the other to hold the door open for his sister Mary.

Immediately, he spied the pale pink envelope on the hall table. Three-quarters buried by the rest of the mail and still he saw it.

"Why don't you go on into the living room?" he said to his sister. They'd just come from dinner, where she'd spent most of her time lecturing him on his lack of social life. He hadn't been on a date since he walked away from Lisa three months ago. "I'll be there in a minute to light the fire and pour the brandy."

"Okay, but don't be long," Mary urged.

"I'll be right there," he answered vaguely, already speculating on the contents of Lisa's letter. Pulling the pink envelope from the pile, he spied the postmark, November first. She'd conceived seven months ago.

He hesitated before opening it as he always did. How like Lisa to want to share her pregnancy with him. She probably thought she was easing his exile when, in truth, the letters were sheer torture to read. They brought her closer to him, but with each one he felt the separation between them more acutely.

Damn his promise.

He'd given her the time, the space, the peace she'd asked for, and it was harder than he'd ever thought it would be. Each day he struggled with the need to see her. The sunshine in her hair, the sparkle in her eyes, the swollen evidence of their child.

Sometimes he'd read one of the letters, and he'd feel so close to her he'd long to give her a call. He didn't. It wouldn't be fair. He still choked at the thought of commitment, and feeling that way, he couldn't justify breaking his word.

He spent a lot of time thinking about the past, contemplating the future. In the meantime, he lived the present day by day.

"Jared?" Mary called. "Are you coming? Mother's been really worried about you."

Jared looked up, frowning at being disturbed. "In a minute." He bent again over the letter.

When Lisa's first letter had arrived, he'd been in a raw state. He'd wondered, violently, if she'd sent it to torment him, just as Beth would have done.

"Come on, Jared." Mary had come back into the hall and hooked her arm through one of his. "I've poured our drinks. Let me tell you about my friend Erika. I'm sure you'd like her."

Jared allowed her to lead him into the living room. He sat on the couch and switched on the lamp.

Mary planted her hands on her hips and sent him an exasperated look.

He didn't see it.

He was too busy tearing off the end of the envelope, pulling free the single sheet of matching pink paper.

Slowly he read, absorbing the nuances. This week she wrote less about how it felt to be pregnant and more about the experience of being pregnant. Strangers approached her spontaneously, and acquaintances talked to her as if they were long lost buddies.

The couch beside him depressed with Mary's weight. "Is something wrong? What are you reading?"

"Huh?" Brooding, he let the letter drift forward to land, written side down, on his chest. He easily recognized Lisa's feelings of isolation.

A soft kiss buzzed his cheek. "Good night, bro."

Blinking, he focused on Mary. "Are you leaving?"

She shook her head in fond frustration. "I love you, Jared. Good night."

"Good night."

Picking up the letter, he read through it one more time. Beneath the written words deeper emotions were revealed. He got the impression Lisa felt as if she was on public display. His first reaction was guilt. He should be with her.

No, he denied, reminding himself he'd wanted to stand by her. He'd even offered to open his home to her. Her rejection still stung.

If Lisa wanted to end her loneliness, she'd have to come to him. She had his number. All she had to do was call.

"Zack." Lisa's greeting held surprise when she answered a knock at the door and found Jared's chief security officer standing there. "Please, come in. What brings you here?"

"I came to see how you're doing and to find out if you need anything." Zack crossed the threshold, his black gaze making a brief sweep of her home, committing the contents to memory. Not for a minute did she doubt he'd be able to tell her, without looking again, that roses decorated the ceramic teapot on the island counter separating her kitchen from the living room.

She liked Zack. She liked his patience and strength, but those were always the second impression she had of him. His sheer size overwhelmed a person's first reaction. At six foot four, with shoulders over two feet across, he intimidated. And those midnight-dark eyes saw everything. In spite of the fact that he worked for Jared, Lisa felt he'd been on her side from the beginning, and she was glad.

"I'm fine," she informed him. Gesturing toward an overstuffed chair, she invited him to have a seat.

"Good." He sat back in the comfortable chair, his long legs sprawled in front of him. "How are the plans for the exhibition going? It must be getting close."

"Less than two weeks now, on the first of December." Lisa lowered herself into a corner of the couch. "Everything is on schedule. Still, I'd be a nervous wreck if I didn't have Ashley. She takes care of every little detail. All I do is paint."

"You don't fool me." Ashley entered the room. She'd obviously heard their conversation as she came down the hall. "You like to pretend you're the simple, artistic type, but I know better. You're the hard-boiled accountant type, not happy unless you've got all the facts and figures at your fingertips. Zack." Belatedly, she acknowledged the seated man.

"Ashley."

Lisa watched them, amused to see them sizing each other up. As far as she knew, this was the longest either of them had been civil to the other. The air fairly sizzled between them, but she didn't even consider the possibility of matchmaking. Her recent experience had been too traumatic.

She decided to take pity on them and end the sudden, stilted silence that had fallen over the room. A playful urge to tease, however, wouldn't be denied.

"Zack, would you care for anything? Coffee, a soda, Ashley?" She paused, and black eyes narrowed their focus on her. Lisa smiled at him and continued speaking as if Ashley's name was meant to be the first word in a new sentence, and not the last word in the previous one. "Would you like something?"

"I'll get it. Zack?"

"A soda, please."

Ashley circled the counter into the kitchen. Lisa heard the loud banging of ice trays, and smiled, pleased at having unnerved her friend. She turned her gaze back to Zack, only to find his intense, knowing eyes fixed on her. Unrepentant, she grinned.

The baby chose that moment to give her a particularly vicious kick. She winced and rubbed her belly, shifting into a position she hoped the baby would find more comfortable.

"Serves you right." A witness to her restlessness, Zack guessed the cause and extended his arm, the large palm of his hand suspended over her stomach. "May I?"

Touched by his interest, Lisa nodded. She took his hand and guided it to where he'd be able to feel the baby's movements.

Her heart turned over when he looked at her and smiled. She'd never seen him grin before. His smile had a boyish quality that stole away a person's fear of him.

It occurred to her she'd never had the opportunity to share such a moment with Jared. The thought hurt. With an effort, she pushed the sadness aside and forced an answering smile.

"Rambunctious, isn't he?" She referred to the baby's activeness. "Sometimes I think he's doing aerobics in there."

"Jared says the baby moves often."

His words startled Lisa. Her eyes widened, the smile slowly faded from her lips. How could Jared know?

"Jared?"

"From your letters. He can't talk to anyone else, so he shares his baby news with me. I don't mind."

Lisa stared at him in an uncomprehending daze. Jared had her letters? He'd read them? No, it wasn't possible. "I don't understand. I never mailed any of the letters. How?"

"I sent them." Ashley stood just inside the room, a tray of drinks in her hands.

Shocked, Lisa blinked, trying to assimilate what she'd heard, what she saw. Ashley's frozen posture and stricken expression evidenced her guilt.

"No." Lisa whispered the instinctive denial. A deep sense of betrayal choked off her ability to speak. She couldn't breathe. She couldn't think. Not Ashley. Her mind, her heart kept rejecting the possibility.

Every last drop of color had drained from Ashley's cheeks. For an endless minute she remained utterly still. She, too, seemed to stop breathing. When she walked forward and set the tray down on the coffee table, the dishes rattled. Testimony to her shaken state. She wrung her hands once, turned and perched on the edge of a chair.

"You sent the letters?" Lisa watched her, agonized with her, and waited. "Why?"

There had to be an explanation. She'd trust Ashley with her life. But now, she wondered, had she trusted her with her heart, only to lose?

At Ashley's continuing silence, a deep, heavy pressure compressed Lisa's rib cage. Emotions bombarded her. In her confusion, it became impossible to separate them, but she recognized embarrassment, betrayal and a building anger. "You don't even like Jared."

"I didn't do it for Jared. I did it for you."

Bemused, Lisa shook her head. "For me?"

"You love Jared, I love you. It seemed the thing to do."

"Because I love Jared, you betrayed our friendship?"

Ashley flinched. "That about covers it, yes."

"Don't be flip about this, Ashley, please."

"I'm not. Believe me, I'm not. I came across the letters one day, and they were so beautiful. I thought if only Jared could read them, he'd come back to you. And you'd be happy again."

"How many...how long have you been sending them?" Lisa dreaded the answer.

"One a week for the last month and a half."

Lisa closed her eyes then opened them to stare at Ashley. "You don't know what you've done. I made him promise to leave me alone. What must he think?" But Lisa feared she knew. He probably thought he had the proof he needed to label her another Beth. A manipulative, tormenting bi—

She pressed two fingers to her lips to cut off the offensive word. Struggling to her feet, she turned. "Zack, I'm sorry you had to be a part of this."

He rose to stand beside her, enfolding her in a quick hug. "I'm sorry, too. I'd never have said—"

Lisa shushed him. "I know. It's not your fault."

Uncertain and concerned, Ashley also stood. "Lisa?"

Lisa couldn't reassure her, the betrayal was too new, too upsetting. "I'd...like it if you'd leave now."

"But..."

"Come on, Ashley." Zack took her by the hand and led her to the door. "I'll walk you to your car."

Not waiting to watch their departure, Lisa went to her room. She needed to lie down and think about what to do next.

In a foul mood, Jared approached the front doors of his office complex. He hadn't slept well. Hell, who was he kidding? He hadn't slept at all. He glared through the glass. When he didn't see a security guard, he dug into his pocket for his keys.

The pressure of inserting the key pressed open the door. Jared's eyes narrowed in displeasure. The force of his swing sent the glass door flying inward. He'd walked only a few feet into the building when the guard appeared.

"Good morning, Mr. Steele." The security officer nodded a respectful greeting.

"Timmons. Are you supposed to be on duty here?" Jared demanded.

"Yes, sir."

"And isn't it your duty to remain at your station unless those doors are locked?"

"Yes, sir. I was just helping—"

"I'm not interested in hearing excuses. Report to personnel. I'll see you're replaced here." The matter handled, he brushed past the man and headed toward his private elevator.

"But, sir—"

"I'll inform payroll to expect you." The doors closed on the harsh comment, cutting off his view of the bewildered guard.

An hour later Jared stood brooding, staring out his office window. His behavior shamed him. He'd completely lost all sense of rationality.

And it was all Lisa's fault.

Every day that went by without hearing from her made him that much crazier. It had been eleven days since he'd received her last letter. Why hadn't she written? Was something wrong? Something must be wrong.

He heard the door open behind him and knew Zack had entered the room. He'd been expecting him. The sound of a file being slapped on his desk drew him around to face his friend.

Zack stood with his arms crossed over his massive chest, his legs spread in a bold stance. His whole attitude issued a challenge.

Jared was ripe for the encounter. He inclined his head toward the file. "What's that?"

"It should be my resignation."

"That's a bit dramatic, don't you think?" He rounded the desk to face Zack across the imposing expanse.

"No." Unfazed, Zack lowered his large frame into a chair without waiting to be invited. "I hire and fire my men, Jared. It's written into my contract. If you had a complaint, you should have come to me."

"Is that what this is?" Jared fingered the folder in front of him. "A copy of your contract? You shouldn't have gone to the trouble. I called down twenty minutes ago and had Timmons reinstated. He'll get today off with pay and a formal apology."

"I know."

"You know? Then why the rampage?"

"To emphasize what a jackass you're making of yourself."

Jared pierced his friend with a glare. "Thank you. I'm well aware of the fact."

"Are you?" Zack settled more comfortably into his seat. "What are you going to do about it?"

Jared hesitated, thinking, but the answers were no easier to come by just because the question had been voiced. "I swear to the heavens, I don't know." He sat down. "I haven't received a letter from her in almost two weeks."

"Her?"

"That's not funny. You know I'm talking about Lisa. She's never gone this long between letters before. Something has to be wrong, but I can't do anything because I promised. Damn it, I promised." Frustration grated through every word.

In his agitation, he resented Zack's capacity for stillness. Jared felt as if he were fraying apart at the seams, and he knew Zack could sit there for hours and not change his position once. Jared envied Zack's control, the kind of control *he* used to possess, the kind he wanted back.

"What is it you really want, Jared? If you could snap your fingers and have anything you wanted, what would you ask for?"

"I want my child. I want to be near Lisa, to feel the baby move within her, to help her when her belly cramps. I want to know they're going to be a part of my life." Jared spoke passionately, his words coming from the heart. "Do you know, I drove by her house a week ago and waited until she came out just so I could see her? She was beautiful. Her skin had a healthy tan and her hair gleamed in the sunlight. To see her swollen with our child—I can't tell you what that did to me."

"Do you love her?"

"I…care for her."

"But do you love her?"

Jared shook his head. "I don't think I can. Something happened to me a long time ago that killed any ability I had to love."

Zack pointed to Jared's desk. "That's what that's for."

Curious, Jared pulled the file toward him. When he

opened the folder and read Beth's name, he sent Zack a searing look. "Who gave you this name?"

"I can't say."

"You don't have to. I didn't think you approved of my mother interfering in my life."

"I don't. A year ago she asked me to do the investigation. I stipulated that if you were ever to see it, I'd be the one to show it to you. I think the time has come."

Jared tossed the file back across the desk. "Burn it. Beth means nothing to me now."

"Then why aren't you with Lisa and your child?" The question hung unanswered between the two men. "You're a progressive, forward-thinking man. It shows in your plans for the company, in your investments, hell, in your choice to have a child by artificial insemination. It's not like you to dwell on the past." Zack stood and gathered the report up. "Some promises were made to be broken."

Jared's head snapped up, his attention sharpened on his friend. "Why do you say that? You know something, don't you? Tell me."

"It's not my place to tell you." Zack headed for the door. "This time you're on your own."

Chapter Thirteen

Lisa stood and surveyed the scene. Her big night had arrived, the opening of the exhibition. Mrs. Dumond had certainly set out to tantalize the senses. Crystal lights glittered like diamonds overhead, and poinsettias celebrated the holiday season, gracing tiered pedestals around the room.

Waiters weaved through the crowd, offering champagne cocktails. Men and women, beautiful in their evening finery, filled the gallery. Some visited the lavish buffet, others sought the fresh, crisp air of the patio, but most of them, Lisa noted with relief, browsed through the displays.

"Lady, you're hot." Ashley suddenly appeared at Lisa's side, brilliant in satin and sequins. "I've heard nothing but good things about you. And," she emphasized, "I know of at least three sales."

"The show is going well, isn't it? Mrs. Dumond

seems pleased. Thank you for all your help." Lisa squeezed Ashley's hand in gratitude, saddened by the reserve lingering in their friendship. If the incident with the letters didn't stand between them, they'd be hugging each other in joy.

Ashley tightened her fingers in fierce response. "Mrs. Dumond is ecstatic. How are you? You look beautiful tonight, but a little tired."

Tired didn't begin to describe how she felt. Excited, relieved, exhilarated and overwhelmingly exhausted would be a more accurate description, not to mention the nagging backache that had plagued her throughout the day.

Tonight exceeded all her dreams. However, expectations aside, she couldn't help wishing it were over. Because she owed the others, Ashley included, who had helped her reach this point, she stayed. Everyone had worked so hard she didn't want to diminish the moment with negative feelings.

"I'm fine." She finally answered Ashley's question.

Worry still shadowed Ashley's brown gaze. "You would tell me if something was wrong?"

"Of course."

"No. There are no more 'of courses' between us. Promise me, Lisa, you'll let me know if you need anything."

"You're all I have, Ashe, that hasn't changed."

"So, I have your word."

"Yes." Lisa meant what she said. Overall, she felt fine. If that fact changed, if she began to feel stressed, she'd let Ashley know immediately. Not for anything would she put the baby at risk.

"Ladies." Mrs. Dumond breezed up. "You look absolutely radiant tonight. Lisa, black lace over gold silk, stunning. Ashley, that turquoise is gorgeous on you. It complements your red hair beautifully.'' The gallery manager vibrated energy. She was in her element, fluttering here and there, never stopping for more than a minute. "Lisa, you're a smashing success. I hope you've told her, Ashley, we have four confirmed sales.''

"Excellent. I only knew of three.''

"Ralphston and Bond are also doing well. Now, I want you to mingle, Ashley. Lisa, you look a little tired. I'm going to have Rene find you a chair. Sit where the patrons can stop and speak to you.'' A flash of concern briefly showed in the woman's eyes. "Unless you're completely zonked, then go lie down on the couch in the lounge.''

"Yes, ma'am.'' Lisa saluted her.

"None of your sass. Oh my, will you just look at that. Young man!'' She chased after a waiter, whose shirt was coming untucked in the back.

"Four sales, that's good, isn't it?'' Lisa looked to Ashley for reassurance of the show's success.

"Very good. I'm just getting the commission, and I'm thrilled,'' Ashley said confidently. "You do realize you'll soon be in a whole new income bracket. You'll have enough to put a down payment on the house you're always talking about.''

"I received a call from the selling agent the other day.'' Lisa picked up on the oblique topic. "She's had a soft spot for me ever since I asked for permission to paint a picture of the house. You've seen the painting, haven't you?'' She glanced around. "It's here somewhere. Did I tell you the agent took me through the place? It has such character.''

"What did the agent say?'' Ashley's interest perked

up. "Are the owners finally willing to come down on the price? It's about time. You'd think after leaving it on the market for a year and a half, they'd get the hint. Should I write up an offer?"

"The house sold two days ago." The blunt statement failed to hide an underlying sadness.

Surprise, then regret chased across Ashley's features. She understood how upset Lisa was at the loss of the house. "I'm so sorry."

"Don't be." Lisa shifted to relieve the discomfort of a mild cramp. "I always knew it was a pipe dream. But you know—" she came to decision "—I think I'd like to keep the painting as a memento."

She excused herself and made her way through the crowd to the desk where Rene discreetly handled the sales transactions. Absently, Lisa rubbed at an ache low in her back.

"Rene." Slowly she eased her weight onto one of the vacant chairs. "I want to pull a painting from the catalog."

"Sure. Which one?"

"I don't know the number." Lisa summoned the energy to sweep ineffectively at the wisps of blond hair trailing down the back of her neck. She'd worn it up tonight in an attempt at elegance. The escaping tendrils tickled rather than stunned.

"Here, you can use my list."

"Thanks." Lisa accepted the notebook and scanned the titles until she found the one she sought. "It's number eighty-seven."

"Okay, let me see." Rene swung the book back around. "I'll just mark it…oh, it's already sold."

"Sold?" Regret washed through Lisa along with a sense of loss. "Thank you for trying."

"I'm sorry, Lisa." Rene's gaze commiserated, then she frowned. "Are you okay? You look a little pale."

Lisa managed a smile. "Not you, too? Honestly, don't look so worried. I'm fine."

Rene stood and looked around the crowded room. "Let me find you a comfortable chair. Mrs. Dumond asked me to find one for you, but I've been busy with the sales."

"Thanks, I'd appreciate a soft place to sit. I know you're busy, so take your time. I'll mingle. See you in a few minutes."

When she left Rene, she made her way to the painting of the house for one last, farewell viewing. She should never have agreed to include the piece in the exhibition, but it was some of her best work.

The house stood silhouetted, proud and noble, against the background of a setting sun. The brilliant hues enhanced the cream stucco structure, reflecting in some places, shadowing in others. As she'd told Ashley, the place had character. A fence of wrought iron and brick revealed terraced landscaping and a winding, red brick walkway flanked by dozens of rosebushes. The ornate front gate stood open and on the sidewalk a small boy played, his bowed head crowned with dark, curling hair.

"A dark-haired boy. You often refer to the baby as 'he' in your letters. Do you know something you haven't told me?"

Jared.

His voice touched a chord buried deep within her then vibrated out to affect her in many ways, on many levels. Her heart welcomed the sound, her body recognized it to an embarrassing degree, but she cringed at the thought of facing him, knowing he'd read her letters.

She stood rooted to the floor, afraid to turn in case she'd imagined hearing him.

"Lisa? Won't you even look at me?"

Oh God, he was real.

Lisa kept her gaze fixed on the painting. "Why are you here?"

"I came to see you. When your letters stopped coming, I started worrying about you." He spoke softly, his voice reaching her under the muted cheer of the holiday crowd, creating an intimate connection between them.

She knew she should face him when she explained what had happened, but she couldn't bring herself to. "I didn't send the letters, Jared."

A stark silence separated them, the tense moment suspending them from the reality of their surroundings. Lisa waited breathlessly for his response. Not even the recurring, clenching spasms in her tummy disturbed the intensity between them.

"Don't tell me you didn't write the letters, Lisa. I won't believe you. I felt you there with me."

"I wrote the letters," she admitted. "Ashley mailed them."

"Ashley? What's she got to do with this?" Outrage roughened his voice.

"She wasn't aware of your promise to me. She thought the letters might bring us back together. Of course, she was wrong." Lisa cocked her head at an angle, her chin raised. "But you'll leave her alone, Jared. I won't allow you to upset her."

From the corner of her eye, Lisa saw his hand poise

above her shoulder then clench into a fist before disappearing from her view.

Lisa swallowed, shaken by the longing that rushed through her for his touch. She should be glad he hadn't completed the contact, but in her heart she cried.

Why did doing the right thing always have to hurt so much? Because for the baby, for herself, she needed to stand strong against him.

"Ashley had no right to interfere," Jared said tightly.

Lisa could almost hear his teeth grinding together. "Ashley is my family, she loves me, just as your mother loves you. Neither of them should have interfered. They did because they care about us."

"How can you defend them?" Fury darkened his tone.

"I have to. When you love, you take the bad with the good."

She felt the scorching heat of his body and knew he'd stepped closer to her.

"Then why won't you look at me?" His breath fanned the exposed skin of her nape. She shivered in reaction and took a small step forward. Less than half the distance backward and she'd have been in his arms.

"I can't." She swallowed around a lump in her throat. "Please don't ask me to watch you walk away again."

"I don't have to walk away."

"Yes, you do." Lisa's tensed posture caused the ache in her back to spread. The muscles in her abdomen were tightening. She tried to ease the sensation by stroking her stomach. "Unless you can say...you love me?"

His silence lasted so long she feared he wouldn't

answer, so long she almost convinced herself he'd been a figment of her imagination.

"Lisa…"

She jumped when he spoke. Of course, he'd been there all along. If he had left, she'd have felt the emptiness his warmth filled.

"I bought the house for you, Lisa. I want to marry you."

A sudden, harsh contraction gripped Lisa, causing her to lean forward to hug herself. Jared's proposal went unacknowledged as she fought to control the pain. Fear paralyzed her. What was happening? The baby wasn't due for another five weeks.

"Lisa!" Jared instantly surrounded her. One arm braced her shoulders, his head bent to hers, and a large hand covered both of hers where they clutched the precious mound of their unborn child. "What is it? What's wrong?"

"Jared." She grabbed at the strength he represented, entwining her fingers with his and squeezing until her knuckles turned white. Sweat beaded her forehead. "I think I'm in labor."

He paled. "That's not possible. You're not due for weeks yet."

"Tell it," she panted, "to the baby." The words were flippant, but tears were forming in her eyes.

The contraction began to ease then came again just as hard as the first. But, she realized, it hadn't been the first. What she'd thought to be discomforting cramps had actually been labor pains. Try as she might, she couldn't remember when they'd started. Hours ago, she knew that much.

Labor hurt. Every ounce of her strength went into enduring the pain. But worse than the physical agony was the mental anguish. Because of her medical history, the doctor wanted to do a C-section. Something wasn't right, and she feared for her child's safety.

Looking into Jared's strained features, she saw a reflection of her own fear. He shared her apprehension, yet supported her weight so she wouldn't have to. If she had the breath to speak, she'd tell him how glad she felt to have him there with her.

A ringing began to sing in her ears, black spots invaded her vision, and the bones in her legs were dissolving. She recognized the symptoms, knew she was about to faint.

"Lisa?" Urgency echoed in Jared's voice when he felt her weight sag against him. He looked frantically around, seeking help. None appeared. With a curse, he swept her into his arms and headed for the door, intent on getting her out of the crush of people.

Ashley, with Zack close behind her, rushed up to him. "What's happened? Is Lisa okay?"

Ashley's concern penetrated the pain clouding Lisa's mind. With great effort, she lifted her hand and whispered one word. "Hospital."

"We're on our way, sweetheart, just hang in there." Jared hugged her to him and began to weave his way through the gallery. Over his shoulder he explained the situation to Zack and Ashley. "She thinks she's in labor. I'm taking her to the hospital."

"I'll ride with you." Ashley stayed hard on his heels. "She may need me."

Feeling less than charitable toward her, Jared snapped, "You can call her doctor."

"I'll handle the call," Zack volunteered.

"Thanks." Jared stopped and swung to face his friend. He nodded toward his chest. "It's Dr. Wilcox.

The number is in my wallet.'' Jared felt Ashley's eyes on them as Zack removed his wallet from his front breast pocket.

''You carry her doctor's number around with you?'' Ashley asked incredulously.

He fixed her with a glare. ''Of course.''

''Ashley.'' Lisa's weak whisper reached out to them. Ashley clasped her hand, careful to stay out of Jared's path. ''I'm here, Lisa.''

''Stay with me.''

''I'm not going anywhere.''

Jealousy raged through Jared. She'd asked for Ashley, and even though he held her cradled in his arms, she had yet to meet his gaze. He frowned. ''Get the door, will you.''

Ashley cast him a curious glance but did as he requested, holding open the gallery door and then the back door of Jared's Mercedes.

''Put her in the back with me,'' Ashley suggested. ''She'll be more comfortable.''

He shook his head, reluctant to release Lisa, desperate to maintain physical contact with her. ''You drive. I'll hold her.''

''I'm not familiar with this make or size of car, and we need to get to the hospital as soon as possible.''

''Then we'll take your car.''

''Jared, we don't have time for this. I have a two-door sports car. It wouldn't be practical.''

He met her stare for stare over the open door. He saw and respected the anxiety for Lisa showing in her eyes. Still, he resented her claim to Lisa's affections. ''Okay, get in.''

He settled Lisa into the back seat. With exquisite gentleness, he meticulously lowered her head into Ashley's lap. Before backing out of the car, he lightly touched his fingertips to her colorless cheek.

"She's going to be okay. Having a baby is a natural event," Ashley said.

"She has to be." Concern and uncertainty made a prayer of the words. He kissed Lisa lightly then backed out and moved to the front seat.

Zack appeared at the driver's window just as Jared put the Mercedes in gear. "Here's your wallet, you'll need it if you're going to be driving. Dr. Wilcox will meet you at the hospital."

"Thanks."

Lisa moaned.

"Jared," Ashley entreated from the back.

"Go." Zack stepped away from the car. "I'll follow you."

The trip was a nightmare for Lisa, a painful, never-ending nightmare. In her more lucid moments, she worried over her baby's safe delivery. Ashley's presence, the soothing stroke of her hand over Lisa's hair, comforted.

"Ashley." Lisa half whispered, half gasped her friend's name.

At the sound, Ashley looked into her eyes. "Shh. You're going to be okay. We're almost there."

"Jared?" Lisa asked around clenched teeth.

"He's here. He's driving. He wanted to be with you."

Consoled, Lisa closed her eyes but opened them again after a heartbeat. "Forgive me."

"Lisa." Ashley shook her head, a look of anguish crossed her beautiful features.

"I should have trusted you about the letters."

"I was wrong to send them."

"Jared said he felt closer to me when he read them. I felt closer to him when I wrote them. They needed to be sent. You saw that."

"You love each other. You belong together."

A tear escaped to run from the corner of Lisa's eye. "I love him."

"If you could have seen him tonight, the way he looked at you, you'd know he cares."

"He's worried about the baby."

"He's frantic about you."

"He said he bought my house."

"I know. Rene told me he bought the painting," Ashley said.

"No, I mean, he bought the house. At least, that's what I think he meant. Ouch." Lisa gritted her teeth and longed for the pain to end. "How much longer?"

"We're here." Jared's announcement sounded loud after their muted conversation.

As soon as he pulled the vehicle to a stop, he shot out of the driver's-side door and stuck his head, his full upper body, through the back door. "How's she doing? Lisa, honey, we're here." He started to scoop her into his arms, but she stopped him. Instead, he assisted her slow, cautious exit from the car.

"Sore." She licked parched lips. "You always take such good care of me when I'm sore."

"I feel so damn helpless."

She reached up and cupped his cheek in the palm of her hand, maintaining the contact until the strength drained from her arm. "Just having you here makes a difference."

"I want to be with you for the rest of my life."

"Sir, we'll take over now." Two emergency attendants flanked a gurney. They quickly and efficiently arranged Lisa on the mobile equipment then rushed her through the emergency-room doors. Jared retained his grip on her hand, needing to touch her for as long as they'd let him.

Ashley hurried forward. "We're supposed to meet Dr. Wilcox here."

"Check in with reception," one of the attendants advised.

"Ashley?" Lisa groped for her friend's hand. "Promise me, if anything should happen, you'll help Jared with the baby."

"Nothing's going to happen." Ashley denied the possibility.

"What's she talking about?" Jared demanded.

"Please," Lisa insisted urgently as the small group rushed through another set of doors. Things were happening so fast. "Tell them of my love. Promise me."

"Yes, I promise," Ashley vowed. In the next instant a nurse gently but firmly requested she step aside.

"Excuse me, sir, you'll have to make room. You're not allowed past this point." The nurse turned her attention to Jared.

"I'm the father."

"I'm sorry, sir. You'll have to wait. This is an emergency. If she's transferred to maternity, you'll be able to see her there."

"Jared!" Lisa implored when the progress of the gurney forced their hands apart.

"Lisa," he called after her, tried to reassure her. "Everything's going to be okay."

"I love you."

The doors closed, shutting him off from her, preventing any reciprocation on his part. He watched through a window as they wheeled her farther and farther from him. He felt his future slipping away and knew he couldn't let them part this way.

He pushed open the door.

"Lisa! I love you!" His shout bounced off the sterile walls.

In despair he watched the gurney disappear around a corner. Had she heard him? His gut clenched with his need to be with her.

He whipped around into the emergency-room foyer. "Where do I find Dr. Wilcox? I want to be in that delivery room."

A nurse looked up from processing a stack of forms. "That's impossible, sir. Miss Langdon is in prenatal distress. Dr. Wilcox has ordered that a surgery room be prepared. You can't go in—"

"I'm the father of that baby!" Jared broke in, frustrated at the bureaucratic dismissal.

"I understand, sir, but until Dr. Wilcox has assessed Miss Langdon's condition, nobody is allowed in to see her."

"Come on, Jared, let's go to the waiting room. Dr. Wilcox will look for us there."

Jared glanced down at the pale hand Ashley had placed upon his tuxedo-clothed forearm, then up at her face. Compassion for him reflected from her brown eyes. Anger roiled in him, barely restrained. He felt as if he might explode at any minute, but he controlled the urge to lash out. For two reasons. One, she also loved Lisa, and two, if she hadn't interfered by sending him Lisa's letters, he'd have missed out on a large part of his child's development.

And he quite possibly wouldn't be here at the hospital tonight.

"Let's go." He relented, allowing her to lead him

to the emergency waiting room. For a full minute he sat in one of the generic chairs, then he was up and pacing.

He detested the little, boxed-in room. It reminded him of another one just like it where he'd spent hours with his mother and sisters waiting to hear about his father. When the news came that night, it hadn't been good. His father had died of a heart attack.

When he thought back, he didn't recall Beth being with him that night. He didn't remember wanting her to be with him. He hadn't loved her.

He hadn't loved Beth. Yet he'd allowed her to take control of his life by letting her vindictive actions cloud his judgment. Whenever he thought of commitment, he became mired in the past instead of focusing on the possibility of a future with Lisa.

Never again.

He felt a gigantic weight lift from his shoulders. Lisa's love freed him from the destructive clutches of the past. He couldn't wait to tell her. He only hoped she'd be able to forgive him for being such a fool.

His heart stopped when he thought about what his pride might have cost him, what it had already cost him. His heartbeat resumed with a frantic pang at the thought of Lisa struggling to have their child alone.

"Dr. Wilcox." Ashley jumped to her feet as a plump, bespectacled matron entered the room. "How's Lisa?"

"Ms. Todd. Mr. Steele." Her handshake was at once matter-of-fact and gentle. "I just have a minute, but I wanted to brief you on the situation. Lisa is doing fine."

"She passed out a couple of times on the ride here, that's not normal, is it?" Ashley asked.

Jared sent her a sharp glance before refocusing on Dr. Wilcox.

The doctor shook her head, her expression grave. "I've done a sonogram and it showed a cyst the size of a plum has formed on her ovary. We're taking steps to stop the labor. Once that's achieved, I'll determine whether to do the C-section now or wait for the baby to mature further."

The hair on the back of Jared's neck stood on end. "What do you mean, stop the labor? Is that safe for the baby?"

"We use medication to stop the contractions in order to halt a premature birth. Yes, it's safe. However, I wouldn't use it in this case except for the risk to Lisa."

Jared's hands formed into fists. He didn't like the word *risk* associated with Lisa. "What happens if you can't stop the labor?"

"A natural birth could cause the cyst to burst. If that happens, both Lisa and the baby will be at risk."

There was that word again. And the doctor's somber tone spoke of the seriousness of the situation. "You're telling me I could lose them both?"

Again the doctor shook her head. "I'm going to do everything I can to prevent that, Mr. Steele. Let's hope for the best."

The doctor glanced at her watch and prepared to leave. Jared stopped her. "Lisa is everything to me, Doctor. If it comes down to a choice, save Lisa."

Sympathy altered the doctor's expression. "Lisa has instructed us to save the child at all costs. However, we'll endeavor to see them both through this safely. Ms. Todd, Mr. Steele, excuse me."

She made her exit, her white coat flapping behind

her. Jared watched her go, devastated by the blow she'd dealt him. He looked at Ashley. "Why?"

Ashley frowned at him and resumed her seat. "I swear, you and Lisa are two of a kind. Nothing's going to happen."

"Ashley!"

She avoided his gaze for a second then looked him square in the eyes. "Because she loves you, Jared, because she loves the baby more than life itself."

Jared hung his head, humbled by the evidence of Lisa's love.

"There's more." Ashley waited until she had his full attention. "She's awarded you custody of the baby in the event of her death. She said you'd suffered too much to lose another child."

Tears gathered in the back of his throat at this news. His vision blurred, casting Ashley's features into a kaleidoscope of images. Shock must have shown on his face because she hastened to continue.

"Don't look like that. It's only a formality. Lisa and the baby are going to be fine."

Jared prayed she was right. He bent over her and pressed a kiss on her forehead. "Thank you. She has a good friend in you." Turning toward the door, he noticed Zack had joined them, though he couldn't have said when.

Ashley sprang to her feet. "Where are you going?" she demanded. "Don't you dare leave. Lisa needs you."

He stopped and swung to face her. "Do you really think so?" His need for reassurance came close to begging, but he didn't care.

"I know she does." Ashley's quick response consoled him. "Why do you think I sent the letters?"

''That's something else I have to thank you for. You needn't worry, I'm not going far. What I said to the doctor is true. Without Lisa I have no life.''

Jared spent the next twenty minutes standing at the back of the hospital chapel silently praying. Only after he'd promised to care for Lisa and their child with all the love in his heart, did Jared leave to make a long-overdue phone call. He punched in a local number and was quickly connected.

''Hello, Mom? It's Jared. There's something I think you should know. I'm going to be a father.''

Chapter Fourteen

"Lisa?" Dr. Wilcox demanded her attention. "Can you hear me?"

"Yes," she said through gritted teeth.

"You have to calm down. Slow your breathing."

She shook her head fretfully. "I'm trying."

"Don't push. Concentrate, Lisa. You have to concentrate."

"Jared," she whimpered. "I want Jared."

"Lisa, the baby is coming. You have to regulate your breathing, and don't push until I tell you."

Lisa tried, she wanted to do as she was told for the baby's sake, but she couldn't control the panic she felt at being alone. "Please."

"Lisa, honey, it's okay. I'm here." Suddenly Jared was there beside her, taking her hand, blotting the sweat from her forehead.

"Jared?" She clung to him, relieved to have him there with her.

"I'm here, darling. Everything's fine. I love you, and I'm going to help you."

"Stay with me," she pleaded.

"I'm not going anywhere. You're stuck with me for the rest of your life. I'd have the justice of the peace in here now if they'd let me."

"Okay, Lisa, push," Dr. Wilcox instructed.

Lisa strained with the effort while Jared coached her on breathing. He'd read up on the Lamaze technique when she mentioned taking the classes in her letters. Her fingers dug into his, her grip tight enough to cut off his circulation.

"Good girl, now relax," the doctor encouraged. "We're almost there."

Lisa collapsed back on the table. She heartily agreed with the one woman she'd talked to who had smiled through gritted teeth and said that labor was "sheer hell." She wanted to crawl out of her own skin and forget the whole idea of having a baby.

Between deep breaths and waves of pain, she panted and asked, "Why?"

"Why do I want to marry you? Or why now?" Jared did his part to keep up the conversation.

She licked dry lips. "Both," she answered, looking into his blue eyes, seeing his love for her reflected there.

"Because." He started, then stopped at a signal from the doctor. "It's time to push again. That's it. That's my girl." He praised her. "You're beautiful. I love you. I was a fool not to trust you or my own heart. I want you and our child, our children, to be a part of my life always."

"This is it, Lisa. You're doing great. Push," Dr. Wilcox urged.

Lisa felt Jared's strength and love engulf her along with an exciting sense of wonder. The same emotions echoed in his tone as he held her and helped her bring their baby into the world.

"Push, darling. Good girl, that's it, push. I can see our baby. Can you see?" Both hands wrapped around one of hers, Jared brought their joined hands to his mouth and kissed her clenched fingers. "Our baby is here. You're brave and wonderful, and beautiful. He's beautiful." His voice broke. A tear tracked a path down his cheek. "It's a boy, darling."

"Congratulations, Lisa, you have a baby boy." Dr. Wilcox stood upright, the precious bundle in her arms. She passed the newborn to Jared, who held him while the nurse ministered to him, then Jared turned and placed their son on Lisa's breast for her to see.

Lisa blinked the tears from her eyes. Her son. Jared was right, he was beautiful. She felt very clever to have pulled off this miracle. The healthy roar of his wail reassured her, but still, he was so small.

"Is he okay?" She carefully inspected all his fingers and toes.

"He's perfect," Dr. Wilcox said. "Well over six pounds, all ten fingers and toes. Strong lungs. The nurse will take him in a minute and give him his first checkup. But don't worry, he's a healthy baby."

Lisa touched her son's cheek. She sat in a private hospital room propped up in Jared's arms with their baby cradled in hers. "Isn't he magnificent, Jared? What should we name him?"

"He's gorgeous and so are you. How about Justin Todd, after my father and Ashley?"

"Justin Todd, I like that."

Jared covered her hand where it covered their child. He kissed first her forehead and then her mouth. He'd be forever grateful he'd been allowed to share in the birth of their son, and that he'd be able to share in his future. "How are you feeling?"

"Honestly?"

Concern, or was it fear, shot through him. "Of course."

"I'm starving."

Jared stared at her blankly until his mind caught up with her response, then he shook his head ruefully. "You are a wonder. My mother's waiting with the justice of the peace."

Lisa blinked back tears. "You do love me."

"Then you'll marry me?"

Lisa looked into his face, saw the recent fear reflected in his eyes, but it was what she didn't see that convinced her of his love. The barriers were gone. Sometime during the long night, he'd confronted his past and won his freedom.

She smiled into his blue eyes. "Bring on the minister."

Epilogue

"**J**ared." Propped up on her elbow behind him, Lisa ran the tip of her tongue along the rim of Jared's ear, tasting him, tickling him. "Wake up." She trailed a path of kisses down his neck to his collarbone.

He groaned and rolled over to cuddle her in his arms. "Again? Hmm. Start without me, and I'll catch up."

She smiled, not doubting him for a minute. "It was fun tonight, having everyone over for Justin's birthday party. Did you see the way his eyes lit up when he saw the little car your mother got him?"

He grinned against her skin. "Only one and he's already a hot-rodder."

"A real daredevil. Thank goodness Ashley got him a helmet. She and Zack looked so happy tonight. Do you think they'll ever settle down and get married?"

"No meddling." The words were a near growl in his sleep-roughened voice.

"I wouldn't." She glanced over his shoulder at the clock. "It's 12:01. Happy anniversary." She slid her foot over a hair-roughened calf.

Without opening his eyes, he pressed a tender kiss to her forehead. "Is this going to become a tradition?"

"It's our first anniversary, and I'm excited." She wiggled into him, her thigh coming into intimate, caressing contact with him, making him gasp. "Every night with you is exciting."

Jared tilted his head back and peered at her through the dimness. His tone serious, he asked, "No regrets?"

She looked into his eyes, their color indiscernible in the darkness, and knew that her heart, her soul and her mind all held the same answer.

"Honestly?"

He half smiled. "Of course."

"I love you. More today than a year ago when you jockeyed the justice of the peace into my hospital room." She traced his lips, loving their shape, their texture. She never tired of feeling them, kissing them. "The next morning, when I woke up, I didn't regret what I'd done, but I did wonder if I'd made the right decision. I was a new mother and a new wife. I worried that I might have misinterpreted your feelings because I wanted so much for you to love me. But every day you prove your love in unconscious ways, supporting my work, delegating more of yours, caring for the baby. I have no regrets." She paused for a heartbeat. "Do you?"

His answer was to kiss her once, hard and deep. "You're a great mother, a successful artist, a fantastic lover and a terrific wife. What regrets could I have, unless you count being awakened at midnight on our anniversary. What's my surprise? Are you going to promise not to do this again next year?"

"Oh, I don't know," Lisa mused. "With two kids, it may be the only time we can find to be alone."

He went still beneath her. The steady rise and fall of his chest stopped. Only the rapid pounding of his heart told her he understood the significance of her announcement.

Suddenly Lisa found herself buried in the bedding, Jared braced above her. "Another baby?" he asked, his gleaming eyes raking her form.

She nodded, smiling, completely confident of his approval.

A self-satisfied smile lifted the corners of his masculine mouth. "When?"

"Early August." Her fingers laced in his hair and pulled his head to hers. She licked her lips. "I'm glad."

He angled his mouth over hers and whispered, "Me, too," before setting his body onto, into, hers, claiming her mouth, her tongue, her womanhood. "Modern medicine aside, there's a lot to be said for old-fashioned methods."

* * * * *

Silhouette ® SPECIAL EDITION®

presents **THE BRIDAL CIRCLE,** a brand-new miniseries honoring friendship, family and love...

THE BRIDAL CIRCLE

by
Andrea Edwards

They dreamed of marrying and leaving their small town behind—but soon discovered there's no place like home for true love!

IF I ONLY HAD A...HUSBAND (May '99)
Penny Donnelly had tried desperately to forget charming millionaire Brad Corrigan. But her heart had a memory—and a will—of its own. And Penny's heart was set on Brad becoming her husband....

SECRET AGENT GROOM (August '99)
When shy-but-sexy Heather Mahoney bumbles onto secret agent Alex Waterstone's undercover mission, the only way to protect the innocent beauty is to claim her as his lady love. Will Heather carry out her own secret agenda and claim Alex as her groom?

PREGNANT & PRACTICALLY MARRIED (November '99)
Pregnant Karin Spencer had suddenly lost her memory and *gained* a pretend fiancé. Though their match was make-believe, Jed McCarron was her dream man. Could this bronco-bustin' cowboy give up his rodeo days for family ways?

Available at your favorite retail outlet.

Silhouette ®

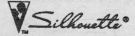

Silhouette® SPECIAL EDITION®

That's My Baby!

Don't miss these heartwarming love stories coming to Silhouette Special Edition!

June '99 BABY LOVE by Victoria Pade (#1249)
A Ranching Family Ry McDermot was capable of caring for his ranch, but was at a loss when it came to his orphaned nephew. Until nurse Tallie Shanahan stepped in to give him lessons on baby love....

Aug. '99 I NOW PRONOUNCE YOU MOM & DAD by Diana Whitney (#1261)
For the Children Lydia Farnsworth would have been happy never to see former flame Powell Greer again. So why was she marrying him? For their godchildren, of course! And maybe for herself…?

Oct. '99 SURPRISE DELIVERY by Susan Mallery (#1273)
Heather Fitzpatrick became irresistibly drawn to the pilot who unexpectedly delivered her precious baby. Now if only she could get her heart—and her gorgeous hero—out of the clouds…!

THAT'S MY BABY!
Sometimes bringing up baby can bring surprises… and showers of love.

Available at your favorite retail outlet.

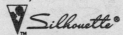

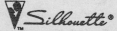

*This August 1999, the legend
continues in Jacobsville*

DIANA PALMER

LOVE WITH A
LONG, TALL TEXAN

A trio of brand-new short stories featuring
three irresistible Long, Tall Texans

GUY FENTON, LUKE CRAIG
and CHRISTOPHER DEVERELL...

This August 1999, Silhouette brings readers an
extra-special collection for Diana Palmer's legions
of fans. Diana spins three unforgettable stories of
love—Texas-style! Featuring the men you can't get
enough of from the wonderful town of Jacobsville,
this collection is a treasure for all fans!

*They grow 'em tall in the saddle in Jacobsville—and
they're the best-looking, sweetest-talking men to be
found in the entire Lone Star state. They are proud,
hardworking men of steel and it will take
the perfect woman to melt their hearts!*

**Don't miss this collection of original
Long, Tall Texans stories...available in
August 1999 at your favorite retail outlet.**

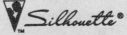